...and Ethan grabbed Simon's hands again. Quickly they rounded the last car and raced down the crowded platform. When it seemed as though they had passed more cars back than they did when they'd come, the boys slowed down and surveyed the scene.

"We never went this far from our train," Bert said, "and we still can't see the end. How come?"

Ethan had no answer to that. They turned around and began to make their way toward the front again.

"Do you see anyone you know?" Bert asked.

"Nope. Where do you s'pose Matron and the girls are?"

The crowd was much smaller than it had been, and the boys looked anxiously at everyone who passed by. Simon tugged at Ethan's hand.

"I saw . . ." he began, but Ethan couldn't listen.

"Wait until we get on the train, Simon, then tell me."

Bert stopped and looked back. "I know we were on this side of the station house," he said. "The train didn't move, so our car has to be here somewhere. Where is everybody, anyway?"

WHISTLE-STOP WEST

by Arleta Richardson

Chariot Books™
David C. Cook Publishing Co.

Chariot Books™ is an imprint of Chariot Family Publishing
Cook Communications Ministries, Elgin, Illinois 60120
Cook Communications Ministries, Paris, Ontario
Kingsway Communications, Eastbourne, England

WHISTLE-STOP WEST
© 1993 by Arleta Richardson for text and Patrick Soper for illustrations

Scripture is quoted from the Holy Bible, New International Version, © 1973, 1978,
1984, International Bible Society. Used by permission of Zondervan Bible
Publishers.

Cover design by Helen Lannis, interior design by Mark Novelli
First Printing, 1993
Printed in the United States of America
97 96 95 94 5 4 3 2

Library of Congress Cataloging-in-Publication Data
Richardson, Arleta
      Whistle-stop west / by Arleta Richardson.
      p.   cm.—(The Orphans' journey; bk. 2)
      Summary: In 1908 eight-year-old Ethan and his three younger siblings
ride an Orphan Train into Nebraska, where they hope with God's help to start a
new life on a farm.
      ISBN 0-7814-0922-5
      [1. Orphans—Fiction. 2. Orphan trains—Fiction. 3. Christian life—
Fiction. 4. Nebraska—Fiction.] I. Title. II. Series: Richardson, Arleta. Orphans'
journey; bk. 2.
PZ7.R3942Wh   1993
[Fic]—dc20

                                                        92-46260
                                                          CIP
                                                          AC

Contents

Dedicated to Ethan's children
John, Bob, Carroll, Clark, Faith, and Hope

The righteous man leads a blameless life;
blessed are his children after him.
Proverbs 20:7

Introduction

The year 1908 was an important one in the lives of the Cooper children, Ethan, Alice, Simon, and Will. In the spring they were moved from Briarlane Christian Children's Home in Pennsylvania to Hull House in Chicago, Illinois, and then put on an Orphan Train for a two-week trip to Nebraska.

Twenty-five girls and boys, twelve from Briarlane and thirteen more joining them at Hull House, traveled west under the care of Matron Daly and Agent Charles Glover. Ranging in age from three to fifteen, the children had very little in common. Some of them remembered no home but the orphanage. Others couldn't recall ever having lived in a building. A few remembered a mother or father in the past, but most had no recollection of anyone ever caring for them.

But there was one thing the children did share. As Charles Glover points out to Matron, "They are survivors. If they weren't, they wouldn't have lived long enough to get this far."

Nevertheless, even the hardiest survivor among them

must have had some anxious thoughts about what lay ahead on this adventure. If a family in a small farming community chose a brother, a sister, or a friend, how would it feel to be returned to the train to go on to the next town? What if the people who took a boy or girl just wanted another farmhand or a maid rather than a son or daughter?

Every effort was made to place the children in suitable homes, and among the thousands of homeless youngsters who rode the Orphan Trains between 1854 and 1929, remarkably few experienced circumstances worse than the ones they had left. For the most part, midwestern farmers lived up to their reputation as "our most solid and intelligent class; possessed of a peculiar warmheartedness."

Ethan, his brothers and a sister, and his friends all embarked on new lives that spring of 1908. They knew there would be good times and bad, happiness and sorrow, security and fear—because that's the way the world is. There would also be God's grace and love and mercy to make the hard times easier and easy times joyful—because that's the way God is.

Arleta Richardson
1992

THE ORPHAN
TRAIN FAMILY

There was nothing, Charles Glover decided, as lonesome sounding as a train whistle moaning through the night. *Whooo, whooo, who, whooo.* It was the letter "Q" in Morse code. What had that to do with approaching a railroad crossing?

Charles turned over on the hard seat that served as his bed. What they needed was a whistle that signaled "help," especially on a train like this one.

The sky was beginning to lighten in the east. If Charles wanted any waking moments of silence, he would have to take them now. Wearily he stood up, folded his blanket, and tossed it overhead. Squinting through the dusty window, he was unable to tell where they were or what the new day promised in the way of weather. Not that it mattered. This train car was home for two weeks, whatever went on in the outside world.

The train lurched and swayed as Charles attempted to

shave in the tiny washroom.

"It's a wonder you don't cut your throat or put an eye out," he said to his image in the mirror. "What are you doing here, anyway?"

This was not what he'd had in mind when he had joined the mission staff to work with Chicago's homeless people. Charles had been excited about being associated with the famous Hull House, founded by Jane Addams. The work was all that he had expected it to be—hard, but rewarding. He had done cheerfully every task assigned to him—too cheerfully, according to his friend Paul.

"You're always so good-natured, Charlie, that you're going to get the assignments others don't want. Do you know anyone else who begs to spend eight months a year on a train with a bunch of street kids?"

"They aren't all 'street kids,' " Charles had protested. "We pick up a lot of children from orphanages and county homes. And it's worth it to see them all placed in good families."

Some days were more worth it than others, Charles admitted as he made his way back to his seat. In the dim light of the long car he could see boys of various ages sprawled on the seats. Unless some had left during the night, there were fifteen of them.

Not much chance of anyone escaping, he thought as he grinned to himself. They were so worn out from the excitement of being on the train that they scarcely moved after the lights were out.

If the nights were quiet, the days were not. These were

obedient children and for the most part well-behaved, but they were boys—given to pushing, poking, and shoving. Nor were they above teasing, Charles recalled as he remembered searching for his tie yesterday, and finding it looped on the door of the girls' car ahead of them.

As he sat down and opened his Bible, Charles breathed a prayer of thankfulness for Matron Daly, who had overall charge of the twenty-five children in their care. Eight of the boys and four of the girls had come with her from the Briarlane Christian Children's Home in Pennsylvania. Charlie had been relieved to find that here was a lady who understood children and was able to direct the activity of a trip like this. As agent for the placement program, he was willing to watch over a group of sleeping boys, but the daily care and discipline of the many young ones was best left in Matron's capable hands.

Charles leaned closer to the window in order to take advantage of all the early light and discovered that his Bible had fallen open to the Book of James. The first verse to catch his eye was most appropriate: "Religion that God our Father accepts as pure and faultless is this: to look after orphans and widows in their distress, and keep oneself from being polluted by the world."

To look after orphans. For over a year Charles's job had been finding homes for children who were wards of the state or who lived on the streets. Each month coaches called Orphan Trains were attached to railroad cars going across the country. At each small town the orphans were lined up in the local church or grange hall, and people in the area were invited to choose a child to take into their homes. So far no child had been returned to the streets because there wasn't a place for him. Folks in the west had opened their hearts warmly and cared for the children whose lives had been hard and lonely.

Across the aisle, Riley Walters sat up and folded his blanket. At fifteen, Riley was the leader of the group. The children respected and liked him, and he did a lot to keep things running smoothly.

Charles smiled at him. "Good morning, Riley. I guess it's time to rouse the troops, isn't it?"

Riley nodded. "Yep. I'd better see that they get washed and brushed before Matron comes in, or we're in trouble. Come on, guys," he called. "Let's get ready for breakfast. Move along, now."

There was a rustle of activity, and heads appeared over the backs of the seats. Another day had begun.

In the girls' car, Shala O'Brien was assisting the little ones with a hairbrush and a soapy washcloth. Her no-nonsense approach to tangles and grimy faces was met with cries of protest.

"Ow. You're pulling!"

"I've got soap in my eye!"

"Hold your head still and your hair won't pull," Shala advised calmly. "Wait until you're dressed to look out the window."

"Where are we, Matron?" Betsy asked. "Are we there yet?"

"We're there all right," Matron replied, "but I'm not sure where 'there' is." She peered out the window at the moving landscape. "It looks about the same as it did before dark yesterday. Here, sit down and put your stockings on. It's time to get breakfast. The boys will be ready for us in a few minutes."

Matron Daly looked fondly at the ten little girls busily preparing for the day. She was grateful for the help from Shala. The twelve year old had come with her from Briarlane, as had Betsy, Alice, and Millie. The other six had joined them in Chicago, along with seven boys. Only four of the children had been requested by a family before the trip began; they were the Coopers.

As she watched Alice putting her new belongings in order, Matron knew she would miss the Cooper children more than any of the others. She was especially attached to nine-year-old Ethan. His concern for his younger brothers and sister was as great now as it had been when the little family arrived at Briarlane a year ago. The year had not been an easy one for them, and Matron prayed that their new home would provide the love and care they deserved.

Shala, Matron thought, could fend for herself wherever she was placed. She was an in-charge kind of a child who wasn't afraid to tackle any job or situation. Betsy was an independent little girl, too. Her sunny disposition would soon win her a place in someone's home. Millie, at age three, was still a baby. Matron well knew that babies were easiest to place, and little girls often had the advantage over little boys in looking irresistible.

The train was slowing, and the girls rushed to the

windows to see where they were.

"We're going to stop, Matron. Do we get out here? Is someone waiting for us?"

"Not yet. Mr. Glover said it would be several days before we come to towns that are expecting us."

"Are you sure they know we're coming?" Eight-year-old Trudy looked anxious. "Did someone tell 'em?"

"Sure they did," Shala answered for Matron. "It's right there in the paper, see?"

"I can't read. I ain't never been to school yet."

"Never been to school! What orphanage were you in that they let you stay home from school?" Shala stared at Trudy in disbelief.

"Weren't in no orphanage," Trudy replied. "I lived in a walk-up with my ma until she died. Then the Mission said I could go on the train."

"Oh. Well, look. I'll read it for you." Shala picked up the newspaper and read the advertisement headed "Notice."

Wanted: Homes for Children

Children of various ages and both sexes will be arriving on the Orphan Train this week. These children are well-disciplined and self-reliant. They must receive education, religious training, and good treatment in every way as members of the family. Distribution will take place at the local hall. Friends from the country please call and see them. Merchants, farmers, and friends generally are requested to give publicity to the above, and much oblige.

C. Glover, Agent

"What's self-reliant mean?" Trudy asked.

"It means you can take care of yourself."

Trudy nodded. "I can do that, even if I ain't been in school."

"We all can," Abby broke in. "We've been doing that all our lives."

You have indeed, Matron thought sadly. *Poor little waifs. I hope the rest of your life isn't as hard as the first has been.* Aloud she said cheerfully, "The cocoa is ready, girls. Wanda, you bring the bread and Nell can carry the jam. Don't forget your mugs. Walk carefully now. The train is gaining speed again."

Shala went ahead to open the doors, and Matron followed with the big kettle of steaming cocoa.

Alice closed her eyes and clung to Betsy as they crossed the narrow bridge where the two cars were coupled together. She dared not look down at the swaying metal beneath her feet. The wide cracks revealed the rushing earth below them, and the wind whooshed their skirts out. The girls' car went one way and the boys' car went the other. What if the two were to come apart while they were in the passageway? The possibility was horrible to consider, and Alice was relieved when the journey was completed. The children were free to come and go between the coaches during the day, but Alice preferred to make the crossing only when it was absolutely necessary. She felt safer in the same car with Ethan.

"All right, children. Line up. Little ones first, please. Get your bread and jam and sit down. I'll bring the cocoa to you."

Very quickly thick slices of bread, each spread with a generous spoonful of jam, were handed out. With Charles carrying the kettle, Matron ladled out the hot drink at each seat.

"Arthur will pray for us this morning," Charles directed, and Arthur shouted out the blessing.

"For what we are about to receive, we thank You, Lord. And help us not to spill. Amen."

In spite of the petition and the best intentions, there were mishaps as mugs reached small mouths just as the train lurched. Matron was ready to mop up with a towel.

"If this is the worst that happens, we'll be blessed," she said. "I've never seen twenty-five clean children together in one place in my life."

"We're in Iowa now," Charles told her. He pulled the watch out of his pocket. "Should be getting into Davenport within the hour. The train will be stopping for coal and water, so we'll have twenty or thirty minutes there. The children can get out of the car and run a little."

Matron looked alarmed. "Get off the train? This is a big station, isn't it? What if we lose someone?"

"We've never lost one yet," Charles assured her. "I'll pair them off so that no one is ever alone. They won't leave the area; there's too much to see here. I think we can put Riley and Shala in charge, and we'll keep Millie and Will with us."

Matron agreed that some exercise other than climbing the seats and running the aisles was necessary for the children. Nevertheless, she determined to keep a sharp eye on her little group.

"I'll be picking up food for today and tomorrow," Charles continued. "We've found that even a dollar a day for each child to eat in the dining car is too much."

The question of feeding everyone for two to three weeks on the train had been considered before leaving Briarlane. It was not practical to carry a lot of food from the home; there would be no place to keep it fresh or to cook it. Matron Daly was pleased to discover that these details had been arranged by Agent Glover.

He is a young man, she wrote to Mr. and Mrs. Lehman at the orphanage, *but remarkably efficient. We are to have a small kerosene stove to heat some foods, and of course water for washing and cleaning up. Each child has his own plate, mug, and tableware, and they all wash their own in hot soapy water after each meal. No one has complained, since the whole trip seems like a picnic to them.*

There is one hot dish at dinnertime, heated on the stove, and cocoa for breakfast. I shall try to fix oatmeal some morning, to be served in the mugs. We are able to purchase a day's supply of milk, fresh fruits, bread and rolls, and such vegetables as can be eaten out of hand or cooked in a stew. The children are all well, for which I

thank the Lord. They get on together with very little
fussing, for there is much to see and talk about.
    The boys and girls who joined us in Chicago are
street dwellers and have never been out of the big city.
Together with our twelve, who had never been in a big
city, we have an interesting group.

By the time breakfast was over and morning prayers
were finished, the train had begun to slow down for the
station in Davenport. When they learned that they were
allowed to get off, the boys and girls were beside themselves
with excitement.
    "Stay together with your partner," Charles instructed
them, "and don't get out of sight of our coaches. When it is
time to reboard, I'll blow this whistle three times. Come at
once to the door where I'm standing. Do you understand?"
    Heads nodded and anxious eyes watched for the big
train depot to appear. The Briarlane children were not used
to so much noise and so many people rushing about. Even
Riley and Shala looked a bit nervous when the train
stopped and the crisscrossed grating on the steps was
pushed aside.

SIMON'S STORY

Ethan Cooper jumped to the platform and turned to lift four-year-old Simon down from the big steps. Steam still rolled from under the railroad coach, and the huge wheels with bent arms that turned them seemed dangerously close.

Simon clung to his older brother as rushing feet and thunderous noise whirled around him. He looked about frantically for Matron.

"Ethan!" he shouted over the din. "Have we lost Alice and Will?"

"No," Ethan assured him. "Matron has Will, and Alice is with Shala and the other girls. You just stay with me."

Bert grabbed Simon's other hand, and the three boys joined the crowd surrounding the train station.

"Remember we have to stay in sight of our cars," Bert said. "We don't want to get too far away."

Ethan glanced back the way they had come.

"We won't have any trouble. Our cars are the last two on the train. Let's watch what they're doing here."

They stopped in front of a car that had no windows. "I wouldn't want to ride in there," Bert said. "You'd never know where you were going. Looks hot, too."

"That car doesn't carry people," Ethan informed him. "I think it has baggage and stuff."

As they watched, the big doors slid open and long flat wagons moved into place beside them. Soon objects of every description began to appear. Men on the train threw bundles, boxes, and suitcases off to be caught by others on the ground and placed on the wagons. Trunks were lifted down, and a crate of squawking chickens found a place beside them.

"Wow!" Bert breathed. "How does anyone ever get their stuff back? I'm glad we didn't put ours in there."

Ethan nodded. "See up there? That's the mail car. Look at all those bags of letters!"

Still dragging Simon between them, the boys dashed to the car ahead. They stood watching as big canvas sacks were tossed off the train and onto wooden trolleys. There seemed to be no end to them, and here again cartons tied with rope and crates holding large objects were unloaded.

"Wouldn't you like to know what's in all those boxes?" Ethan said. "I guess you can send anything but people through the mail."

At the front of the long train, past the station house, more activity was taking place. A huge chute swung out over the car behind the engine, and coal poured down it with great speed. Black soot flew up, and the noise was deafening. The boys watched in fascination as the coal car filled up.

A torrent of water was poured into the boiler attached to the engine.

"That's what keeps her going," a voice shouted over the racket, and strong arms scooped Simon from the ground. It was Riley, and he placed the little boy on his shoulders. "Now you can see better."

He could indeed, and what Simon saw caused his eyes to widen in amazement. The track on the other side of their train was clearly visible to him. Another train, headed toward the east, was standing on that track. He clutched Riley's hair and hung on as he gazed openmouthed.

"Ethan," he hollered, "There's—"

But Ethan couldn't hear him. Simon continued to talk, but his words were carried by the wind to join the rest of the hubbub around them. No one answered him or seemed the least bit interested in what he was saying. By the time Simon was lowered to the ground, he had decided to say no more about what he'd seen. They wouldn't believe him anyway.

Riley disappeared into the crowd, advising the boys to start back toward their coach.

It was warm on the platform, and Simon was tired of being pulled along at breakneck speed. "It's hot down here," he complained. "I can't see anything. Besides, I'm thirsty."

Ethan and Bert stopped to look around them.

"There must be a pump around here somewhere. All

these people have to get a drink once in a while," Bert reasoned.

"There's one," Ethan pointed out. "Right there behind the building." They rushed over to it and took turns pumping the water and drinking from their hands. While the other two drank, Simon stood, swinging his arms back and forth. It felt good not to have them being jerked both ways.

"Watch out, little boy," a voice said behind him. "You almost whacked me in the nose."

Simon whirled around and found himself face-to-face with a girl no taller than he was.

"I'm not a little—" he began, then stopped and stared. This was no girl. She was small, to be sure, but she was dressed in lady's clothes, and her face appeared to be as old as he remembered Ma's to be. Simon opened his mouth to ask who she was, but a sudden *whoo, whoo* from the train prevented it.

The tiny lady disappeared, and Bert and Ethan grabbed his hands again. Quickly they rounded the building and charged down the crowded platform. When it seemed as though they had passed more cars back than they did when they'd come, the boys slowed down and surveyed the scene.

"We never went this far from our train," Bert said, "and we still can't see the end. How come?"

Ethan had no answer to that. They turned around and began to make their way toward the front again.

"Do you see anyone you know?" Bert asked.

"Nope. Where do you s'pose Matron and the girls are?"

The crowd was much smaller than it had been, and the boys looked anxiously at everyone who passed by. Simon tugged at Ethan's hand.

"I saw . . ." he began, but Ethan couldn't listen.

"Wait until we get on the train, Simon, then tell me."

Bert stopped and looked back. "I know we were on this side of the station house," he said. "The train didn't move, so our car has to be here somewhere. Where is everybody, anyway?"

While they stood, uncertain which direction to take, three shrill blasts from a whistle sounded behind them. Mr. Glover stood on the step, waving. "Come on, boys, this way. Hurry!"

Simon's feet fairly left the ground as they raced toward the open door. He was lifted aboard, and Bert and Ethan clambered after him as another *whoo, whoo* sounded and steam puffed around them. *Chug, chug, chug. Chug, chug, chug.* The train shuddered and shook and gathered speed as the boys fell into the nearest seat, panting heavily.

Riley stood and surveyed them with disgust. "I rounded everybody up down there by the coal car and told you to get back here. Where'd you go?"

"We stopped to get a drink," Bert gasped when he could speak again. "How come they moved our car?"

"What's the matter with you, boy? This car was right where we left it! We better not let you off again if you can't find your way back." Riley sounded annoyed, because he had worried about the boys.

"We was the last one in line," Bert maintained stoutly,

"and now there are some behind us. How come?"

Charles Glover overheard them. "The boys are right," he said. "I didn't think to warn you about that. The train takes on more cars between cities and carries them short distances. When we reach the first town in Iowa where we will stay overnight, our cars will be unhitched, then picked up by the train going west the next day. We can't tell coaches by where they stand in line. We'll need another way."

"I'll tie a scarf on the bar beside our door," Matron said. "Then you can't miss it. All right, girls. Let's go back to our car and get ready for dinner. Wash up, boys. We'll be back shortly."

By the time dinner was over, the train was speeding across the open prairie again. The smaller children slept, and the older ones, seeing nothing new to keep their attention, were staying busy as best they could. Bert watched as Ethan sketched a picture on a tablet balanced on his crossed legs.

"Looks just like the station house," Bert commented. "Where'd you learn to draw like that?"

"I don't know. I just always could. I used to make pictures in the dirt back home, and Ma always knew what they were. This is better, because I can keep them to look at later."

Bert picked up a box of drawing pencils that lay on the seat beside Ethan. "Mr. Smalley knew just what to give you for a gift, didn't he?"

"I'd rather have these than anything," Ethan replied.

"He was a good teacher, wasn't he? I guess he was sorry to see so many of us leave Briarlane."

"I 'spect he thought he'd always have us orphans in school," Bert said. "But there'll probably be more to take our place. It was nice of him to give us all something to remember him by."

The boys leaned back and looked out the window. So much had happened in the past week that it was hard to sort it out.

It had all begun with news that twelve children would be traveling on the Orphan Train to new homes in a western state.

"There is a family by the name of Rush who lives in Nebraska," Mr. Lehman had told Ethan. "They want you to come and live with them. You'll have a mother, a father, and an older sister named Frances."

"Are you sure they know that there's four of us?" Ethan had asked anxiously. "They won't just take one and leave the rest of us there?"

"I'm sure. They know that you will all stay together. Mr. Rush has a large farm and a lot of room. I'm sure you'll be happy there."

Bert broke in on Ethan's thoughts. "Remember the day we left on the train to Chicago?" he asked.

"Sure. I've got a picture of it here." Ethan flipped the pages of his drawing tablet back to the beginning. There stood a long train with children climbing aboard. Smoke rose from the stack and steam billowed along the ground. People stood on the platform, waving at the passengers.

"Boy—that looks just like us!" Bert was impressed. "That's good. What else have you got?"

Ethan turned the page. "This is Chicago."

Tall buildings rose in the background, and on one side a blue lake glistened. People crowded the sidewalks, and bridges crossed a river. Bert studied it carefully.

"I never saw such a big city before," he said. "I'm glad we didn't stay there any longer. Where's the Hull House that we stayed in?"

Ethan turned another page and pointed out a big building surrounded by people, trolley cars, stores, and houses.

"Is this where we're going to live?" Alice had asked. "I don't like it here. I'd rather go back to Briarlane."

"We won't be here long, Alice," Ethan had told her. "Just until the train is ready to take us to our real home. Besides, Matron said we'd have a nice surprise here. You wouldn't want to miss that."

The days at the Hull House had been exciting. A large room was filled with clothes for all the children who were going on the train. Ethan and the other boys were outfitted in the grandest style they had ever seen. From the high-buttoned black shoes to the knickers and jacket that completed the suit, every piece of clothing was brand-new.

"I never had nothing that nobody else ever wore before," Bert said. "Do you mean we really get to keep these?"

Matron assured them that they did. "You won't be

wearing them until we meet the people who will give you homes," she said. "It's important to look nice then. They don't want a scruffy-looking child."

While he was dressed in his elegant outfit, Ethan offered to be the doorkeeper for the busy Hull House. He was given permission, and for a day he opened the big door for arriving and departing visitors.

"It was nothing like door duty at Briarlane," he told Bert later. "I didn't have to dust or anything. I just had to open the doors and say 'Good day.' They said 'Thank you, young man' just like I was somebody."

The younger children awoke and demanded attention. Ethan tucked his drawing book and pencils away in his bag, out of reach of small fingers. Simon knelt on his seat beside him and pressed his nose against the window.

"I saw somebody," he announced.

Ethan glanced out at the fields and woods rushing by. There were no signs of life as far as he could see.

"Was it a farmer?" he asked the boy.

"Nope. A little bitty lady."

"There's no ladies out there, Simon. We're way out in the country."

"I saw her. She said 'Watch out, little boy. You almost smacked me in the nose.' "

Ethan laughed at him. "Come on, Simon. You made that up. If there was a lady out there, and if she did say something, you couldn't hear from the train. Where'd you get that story, anyway?"

"Not a story," Simon replied patiently. "She was shorter

than Alice and she wore a little bitty hat. But she was old. She had a purse."

"You sure had a good dream, Simon," Bert said. "What happened to the lady?"

"I don't know. You made me go away. But I never hit her," he added quickly. "I just almost did."

Ethan shook his head. It wouldn't do any harm to let Simon believe his story. If he imagined he saw a lady his own size, it couldn't hurt anything. The boys decided to play checkers with the game Mr. Smalley had given to Bert, and the afternoon passed quickly.

They had not gone through any more large towns before it began to get dark. A supper of bread and milk with fresh fruit that Charles had bought in Davenport was eaten with a good appetite. Matron surprised them by handing out cookies for dessert.

"How did you bake these on that little stove?" Philip wanted to know. "I didn't smell them."

"These were baked at Hull House," Matron said. "I saved them to eat a few at a time. Two apiece tonight and more tomorrow."

"Too bad they can't last like the cakes the widow in the Bible made," Riley said. "These are good."

"What kind of cakes?" Trudy asked. "How long did they last?"

Matron sat down and smoothed her apron. "You never heard that story? Well, I'll have to tell you about it. There was a widow who had a young son," she began.

"Was he an orphan?" Trudy interrupted.

"He was fatherless," Matron said. "His mother was caring for him alone."

"Just like me," Trudy nodded.

"Yes, just like a lot of you," Matron agreed, and then continued. "A stranger named Elijah came to town, and he asked if she would bake a cake for him.

" 'Oh, sir,' she said, 'I would gladly do it, but I have only enough meal and oil for one cake to feed myself and my son. That's all the food we have in the house.'

" 'Bake one for me first,' Elijah said, 'then you can feed your son. I've come a long way, and I'm hungry.'

"The widow felt sorry for the man, so she did as he asked. She took the cake outside to where he sat and gave it to him.

" 'God will bless you,' Elijah said. 'You will not run out of meal or oil as long as you need it.'

"The widow returned to her house and found that what Elijah had said was true. God provided for her needs from then on." Matron smiled at Trudy. "We know that He will provide for our needs too, because he promised that He would take care of His children. Now, let's have evening prayers and get ready for bed."

The lights were soon out, and Ethan and Bert curled up in their seats at the end of the long car. It had been an exciting day, and the boys were tired. They were asleep almost at once.

In the night, the train slowed, then jerked to a stop. Ethan roused enough to turn over. He would have gone right back to sleep, but a sound like a low roar began right behind his ear. Wide awake now, Ethan sat up quickly and listened. Yes, there it was again. There was the noise of heavy feet stomping, and Ethan pulled his blanket around him and stared into the darkness. He reached out and shook Bert, who lay on the seat across from him.

"Bert! Bert!" he whispered. "Wake up! There's something in here!"

Bert opened his eyes. At that moment, the train began to roll again, with the usual grinding of the wheels and puffing of steam.

"There's a lot of us in here," Bert said grumpily. "How come you woke me up to tell me that?"

"It's not us," Ethan said. "It's something making a big noise. Can't you hear it?"

"I just hear the train," Bert replied. "You're as bad as Simon. Go to sleep."

He closed his eyes, and Ethan lay down again. The *chug-chug* of the train was familiar, but he had heard something else. He knew he had.

3

A NEW FAMILY
WAITS

As the Orphan Train whistled and clattered through the night on its way west, a small country town in Nebraska lay quietly in sleep. Earlier that day its inhabitants had gathered around the post office and read with interest the notice tacked up there.

"Wonder how many children they have on that train?"

The man who spoke had read the information slowly and carefully. His question was directed to anyone standing around who wished to answer.

"Don't know as I approve of giving children away," someone else commented.

"Doesn't look to me like taking in a stray cat. Look what you have to do. Feed and clothe 'em, send 'em to school and church, and treat 'em like family."

"Might be worth it to get a good, strong boy to help out on the place."

"I'd think awhile before I'd take a strange child into my home, I'll tell you. Especially when they're part grown. How do we know where they came from?"

"We know." The postmaster entered the conversation. "They come from orphanages and off the streets. The cities can't take care of all of 'em. Probably some been in trouble with the law, too. Could be we'll be taking in their problems."

"If everyone stayed home and took care of their own children, they wouldn't be in this fix."

"Come on, now, Rhody. That ain't fair." The miller's wife spoke out. "Some folks in the city die sooner than we do out here. What happens to those poor little ones when they got no parents left? You can't say that's their fault. Most of us has lots of space and enough food for another mouth. It won't hurt us to help out. I, for one, intend to be here to look them over."

Heads nodded in agreement.

"I think I'd like a little girl. She'd be real company for me out there so far from town. The menfolk are gone all day, and I can't say as they're much good when they are home. For company, that is."

"A young'un would be nice. Think I'll speak to Ed about it tonight. When does it say they'll be here?"

Several bystanders peered at the sign again. "Looks to me like a week from tomorrow. We got time to think it over."

The group began to drift away from the post office, and only those who chose that spot to spend their day were left. One of them called out to a departing farmer.

"You planning on trying for another orphan, Chad?"

"We're thinkin' on it," the man replied shortly. Without a backward glance he climbed onto his wagon, clucked to the horse and moved down the road. The others silently watched him out of sight.

"Pity the orphan that gets picked by him."

"Oh, I don't know. He's fair. He'll provide for 'em and send 'em to school."

"If it's a girl. If it's a boy, Chad'll send 'im to school when he can't think of something else for 'im to do."

While these dire predictions were being voiced, Chadwick Rush was making his way home. He had not entered into the conversation with his town neighbors. There would be talk enough when the train arrived, he knew. The countryside went by unnoticed as he reflected on the last few years of his life.

Chad Rush was a successful man by anyone's standards. He had, by the age of thirty-five, managed to acquire more property than any of his neighbors and to make it produce more abundantly than the areas around it. He had a sharp eye for a bargain, whether it be in land to homestead or equipment to run it. He was known by his neighbors as a "hard man."

While still at home on his father's farm, Chad had met Manda Scott. She seemed to be a steady, industrious girl, from a good family, and was willing to start a home of her own. Chad decided it was a good idea to marry her, especially when his father offered them a parcel of land to get started on. It wasn't long before Chad learned that

Manda was as determined as he was, and not always in the same direction. There were stormy days ahead.

The first house to be built, for example, should have been a simple affair. It was not.

"I'm not going to work in a kitchen the size of a henhouse," Manda declared. "There has to be a separate pantry and a cold room. Take the partition out between here and the parlor, and it'll be about right."

"We don't need a house that big for the two of us," Chad protested. "I can't spend all spring working on it. I have to get my crops in. You can make do until I have time to add on."

"I don't 'add on' to anything," Manda snapped. "I do it right the first time. Now, are you going to put up a decent house, or will I call Pa to do it for me?"

Chad had put up a "decent house," and in the years that followed, had constructed several others, each more elaborate than the last. Manda took a critical view of all of them.

"Seems to me you could have made that bedroom a little bigger."

"Two windows will never let enough light into that north room."

"Should've gone for the paint myself. I could have found a better color than that."

"I don't like the way the curtains hang. We'll have to take time to go to town today."

Eventually Chad began to spend as much time as possible in the fields or exploring possibilities for acquiring new land.

The state of affairs in the Rush home did not proceed without comment from the neighboring wives.

"Have you seen the new linoleum Manda Rush has in her kitchen? Must have cost at least five dollars."

"That ain't all. She's having Chad put a pump in her sink! Says she's not about to lug her wash from the well."

"Has a hired girl, too. And nobody but them two to look after."

"What she needs is some kids to take up her time. Give her something to do besides chivvy her husband into fancying up that house."

"He could say no. That's what my Horace would do if I tried it."

"Hah. You don't say no to Manda without living to regret it."

One neighbor tried to find a bright spot in the dreary picture. "They are church comers, and they tithe regular."

"Takes more'n that to make you act like a Christian," sniffed another. "And as for children, it's the Lord's blessing they ain't got none. Them two hasn't got a heart between 'em."

Chad Rush was not aware of his neighbors' opinions. He did feel that life had dealt him some raw deals, and that he had the privilege of staying out of everyone's way and minding his own business. He wasn't downright unfriendly, but he wasn't the most sociable member of the community, either.

Now as his horse plodded down the dusty road in the direction of the Rush farm, Chad thought about the notice at the post office and sighed. One week more, and he and Manda would have something else to scrap over. He knew that's how it would be. Chad's shoulders drooped, and he felt the weight of sadness that had hung over the place in recent months.

It had all begun five years ago, on a Sunday morning in church.

"We've had a letter this week from back east," the preacher announced. "As you know, our church sends support to a children's orphanage in Pennsylvania. They write once in a while to tell us how our money is used. I thought you might like to hear about what they're doing now." He proceeded to read the letter.

Money has been received from many areas of the church, some as far west as Nebraska and Colorado. We do appreciate the sacrifices these good folks have made to keep Briarlane going. This spring we have been able to paint the barn, repair the steps to the main building, and purchase two cows. Our older boys assist with the farm work, and the girls help with cleaning and looking after the younger children.

At this date we have thirty-two children to care for, with a staff of seven dedicated people. Three orphans have been adopted this year, and many others are available. We ask that you would prayerfully consider taking a boy or girl into your home. Godly parents can change the lives of these children who have been left homeless through no fault of their own. If you are interested, please contact George Lehman, Director of Briarlane Christian Children's Home.

Chad didn't give the announcement another thought, but on the way back from church, Manda was unusually quiet. Eventually she spoke up.

"We could take one of those little ones," she said. "I could use a girl to help out around the house. Or if we got a boy, he'd be a hand for you on the farm. The way you're taking in property, you'll need more than hired men to run it. Be nice to have someone to leave it to when we're gone."

"Lot of work to bring up a child," Chad replied. "You need to think about that before you take one on."

Manda waved her hand impatiently. "No more than I'm already doing. I cook and clean and wash and sew for everyone who works on the place now. Another one won't make any difference."

"Don't know," Chad said to his father later. "If it will make Manda a little more contented with the place, it'll be worth it. If it gives her something else to complain about, it won't."

In spite of his misgivings, Chad agreed to write to Briarlane for information. In return came a description of an eight-year-old girl.

Frances is a happy, dependable child. She is helpful and intelligent. Both her parents are dead, and Frances and her eighteen-month-old brother, Robbie, were sent here by the state. Could you see your way clear to taking both of them? You will not be disappointed. They are good children who will fit well into any family situation.

"We can certainly afford two, especially when one is just a baby," Manda had declared. "I think we should take them.

If they don't work out, we'll send them back."

Chad flicked the switch over the horse's back to dislodge the flies that swarmed about in the warm spring air. It had been such a day as this that he and Manda had gone to town to board the train for Chicago. They were to pick up Frances and Robbie at Hull House, the way station for orphans going west.

Five years ago. So much had happened in that time, and in spite of the fact that Chad didn't want to remember most of it, his mind continued to play the scenes out before him. . . .

Hull House was in the middle of a huge, busy city. How anyone could bear to live there, Chad didn't know. As they sat in the office, waiting for the children to be brought to them, he was thankful for the open prairies of his Nebraska home. As soon as the business had been completed, he was ready to take the first train back. Not so, Manda.

"How often will we have a chance to look around a big place like this?" she asked. "Leave the children here for another day, and we can see the sights."

See them they did, Chad remembered. By the end of the day he was more exhausted than he would have been after working all day in the fields. City life was not for him. The following morning he departed happily for Willow Creek, Nebraska, with his newly acquired family.

From the beginning Frances clung to him. She was smaller than Chad had expected for an eight year old. Her short brown hair and large, dark eyes gave her an appearance of helplessness and innocence.

"Not very pretty, is she?" Manda commented. "Maybe she will grow out around it."

The baby was ready immediately to love everyone. It was to him that Manda directed all of her attention. This was probably the reason, Chad thought, that he had pampered and spoiled Frances until now, at the age of thirteen, she was sometimes impossible to live with. In fact, it was she who was partially responsible for the events that troubled him today.

When Robbie was three years old, Frances had been left to watch him while Manda was occupied in the house. The girl's attention was on other things, and she didn't try to stop the little boy from walking on the thin ice covering the creek. When she pulled him, shivering, from the water, her biggest fear was the wrath of her mother. Frances delayed taking Robbie to the house as long as she dared. The result was pneumonia, and the following week, Robbie died.

Frances was inconsolable. Manda refused to talk about it. Chad was torn between sadness at the loss of the little boy and his inability to understand his wife and daughter.

Then this April, a newsletter arrived from Briarlane Christian Children's Home. Frances had been the first to see it.

"Papa, this letter says that the home has four children from one family that they want to send west on the Orphan Train. There's one little girl and three boys. I think we should get them. I'd like a sister, and we need a boy to replace Robbie. You'd better write to them before someone else does."

"Four children, Frances? Are you out of your mind?" Manda was not in favor of the idea. "Maybe the two youngest boys, but not all of them. We don't need that many."

Frances cried and begged.

"Life couldn't be any more miserable around here with four more children than it is now," Chad declared after several days had gone by with no peace. "I could use the older boys around the place, and you'd have another baby to spoil."

"If you hadn't given Frances everything she's wanted for five years, it wouldn't be this miserable," Manda grumbled. "You'll go ahead and do it again, I've no doubt. I can only hope someone has already asked for them."

But no one had, and the train was at this moment bringing the Cooper children into the lives of the Rushes in Nebraska. Chad watched his house and barn grow larger as he approached them.

He had one week in which to break the news to Manda that they were going to leave this place at the end of the summer and homestead new territory up in South Dakota. The four new children would have to come with them, of course. Chad's brother would run his place until they returned. Maybe those boys would come in handy to help clear the ground and work on the new land. They might as well be doing that. Chad was sure they wouldn't be likely to improve Manda's temper. That wasn't even a possibility.

4

READY OR NOT

Ethan awoke to the sound of voices in the other end of the coach. He sat up and looked around. On the seat facing him, Bert still slept soundly. The sky was getting lighter, but it appeared to be very early. As he gazed out the window, still drowsy with sleep, Ethan listened idly to Riley and Mr. Glover.

"Are you always awake this early?" Riley was asking.

"Yes. I need to get ready for the day. It's the only time I have to read my Bible and pray before everyone is awake."

"You read your Bible to yourself every day?"

Charles Glove admitted that he did.

"Matron reads to us every morning, and we always have Sunday school on Sunday afternoon," Riley said. "I've heard a lot of the Bible, but I never read it myself."

"It's time you did," Charles told him. "You're old enough to read and understand it on your own."

"Don't have a Bible."

Charles nodded. "I suppose not. But I'll see that you get one before you leave the train. You need to start learning verses. If you memorize them, they have a way of coming back to you just when you need them."

"I do know a few verses," Riley said, "and I remember a lot of stories. But I suppose there's a bunch I haven't heard yet."

Ethan's mind wandered away from the conversation as he recalled the noises he'd heard in the night. He wasn't sure he hadn't dreamed it, but it had seemed real then. As the train chugged around a curve, he looked back at the cars which still followed them. There were three freight cars and one more passenger coach on the end. They must have picked up a lot of mail and baggage in Davenport.

Bert awoke, yawned, and stretched. He eyed Ethan and frowned. "How come you woke me up in the night? Who'd you think was in here?"

So he hadn't dreamed it. Ethan shrugged.

"I don't know. It sounded like someone with awful big feet and a loud voice."

"What'd they say?"

"They didn't say anything—just made a lot of noise."

"You was dreaming," Bert decided. "Nobody else heard it, did they?"

"I guess not. But I was awake enough to wake you up."

Bert couldn't deny that. The boys folded their blankets and headed for the washroom. Matron had promised a thorough scrubbing for that day, so a quick dab of the face and a brush through the hair took care of their preparation for breakfast.

The others were soon ready, and Matron and the girls appeared with hard-boiled eggs, bread, and cocoa. As a special treat, each child was given an orange.

"I was going to save these for noon," Matron told them, "but if you're going to get sticky, do it now before we begin baths. Mr. Glover tells me that we'll reach one of our stopping places this afternoon."

Silence fell over the group, and they looked around at each other anxiously.

"Which one of us is gonna get took, miss?" The question came from one of the Chicago boys.

"I don't know, Pete," Matron replied. "That will be up to the people who come to see you. Do you all remember what we are to do when they take us to a church or a town hall?"

Heads nodded solemnly. Now that the time had come near to be parted from friends and those they depended upon, the children were not as sure about this adventure as they had been.

"As soon as we've had prayers this morning, we'll go over the song together and practice the pieces you're going to say," Matron said. "You will all do just fine."

"I think I'm going to be scared, Matron," Philip said. "What if I forget what I'm s'posed to say?"

"Just look smart," Bert advised him. "Sometimes if you keep your mouth shut, people think you're smarter than you are."

Charles Glover looked at Bert with new respect. This, he felt, was excellent advice.

But Matron quickly reassured the boy. "Don't worry,

Philip. You've been saying it a long time, you won't forget. Here—let me read something to you from the Bible. 'Whatever time I am afraid, I will trust in you.' Who is this One we trust in?" she asked.

"Jesus!" chorused the Briarlane children.

"I don't trust nobody," Arthur stated. "Who's this Jesus fella, anyway? I don't know Him."

The orphanage children looked at Arthur in horror, then back at Matron. What would she do to a boy who talked like that? To their surprise, Matron's eyes filled with tears.

"We want you to know Him, Arthur. He is the Son of God, and He came to earth to die because He loves you."

"Me?"

"Yes, you and all of us."

Arthur looked slowly around the circle of faces. "You ain't stringin' me, are you?"

"Of course she ain't!" Shala was outraged. "It's right here in the Bible! Just look at it for yourself."

"I can't read no Bible," Arthur muttered.

"You neither? Well, never mind. We'll read you the story about Jesus if you want to hear it."

"Yeah, we can even tell it to you," Bert put in. "Ain't you never been to church or Sunday school?"

Arthur shook his head. "Nope. Didn't know there was such a place until Mr. Glover brung me to Hull House. I wasn't there very long, but I heard a story about a man who got beat on by some thieves, and two guys wouldn't help him, and then one did. Was that one Jesus?"

"No," Matron replied, "but he was acting the way Jesus

wants us to act. That was a story that Jesus told to the
people. We'll hear more stories, Arthur, while we're on the
train. And you'll have a chance to go to church with the
new family you live with."

After prayers, the children practiced the song they had
learned to sing to the people who would come to look them
over.

"If I only had a home, sweet home, someone to care for me,
Like all the other boys and girls, how happy I would be!
A kind papa and mama dear, to call me all their own,
This world would be like sunshine if I had a home,
    sweet home."

Everyone sang loudly and as much in tune as possible.
Matron and Mr. Glover agreed that they had done well.
Some of them sang little songs by themselves, or recited
poems that were sure to impress the listeners.

"My name is Nell,
And I can tell
That you are good and kind.
If you will take me home with you,
I'd promise I will mind."

"As you can see, I'm big and tall
And strong as I can be.
You wouldn't have to work so hard
If you had a boy like me."

It was Arthur, however, who won the admiration of everyone with his acrobatics. He walked on his hands, did back
and front flip-flops, and rolled like a ball down the train aisle.

"He don't look like he has any bones," Bert commented. "I wish I could do that."

"You could if you practiced," Arthur told him. "It's better to try it on the grass, though. You need lots of space to learn."

Ethan watched all this activity with interest. There was no reason for the Coopers to recite poems or to perform; they had already been chosen.

"You're lucky," Bert said. "I'd like to know where I'm going."

"I don't know where I'm going," Ethan replied. "Just because they spoke for me doesn't mean they'll like me."

This was the fear of most of the older children. What if the families who chose them decided later that they didn't like them?

Matron tried to reassure everyone. "The Lord has promised to guide us with His eye. He's not going to lead us the wrong way, is He? We're going to trust Him for good homes for all of you. Now, let's make ourselves presentable for our first stop."

The next hour was not enjoyed by everyone. The older boys and girls helped scrub the younger ones. Hair was washed and brushed, and new clothes were put on.

"Matron, I'm not going to have no skin left if Riley don't let up," Pete complained. "Them's freckles he's trying to rub off."

"Mr. Glover, Billy's curling his toes up, and I can't get his shoes on," Philip complained.

Shala scolded Alice. "Now see what you did to your sash! I tied it just perfect and you had to turn it around to look at it!"

Finally, however, everyone was neatly dressed and combed, and Charles Glover looked them over with satisfaction. "As nice looking a bunch of children as I've ever had," he declared. "We'll be proud to show them to the people in Liberty."

Fortunately, the town of Liberty was not far away. The train had began to slow, and as many faces as possible were pressed against the windows. Everyone wanted to be first to catch a glimpse of the station. They spoke together in whispers.

"You're allowed to talk out loud, you know," Charles said. "We want these folks to think they'll be getting real children. You can always hear that kind."

"We've been hearing them for several days," Matron added. "I'll tell the folks how real they are."

"We're scared, miss." A little Chicago boy turned from the window with anxious eyes. "I weren't never scared on the streets, but I am now. What are we going to do with all that space? There's nothin' to hide behind."

"What's there to hide from?" Philip wanted to know. "Is someone after you?"

Arthur looked at Philip kindly. "If you was safe in an orphanage every night, you wouldn't know, kid. We 'uns lived on the street and slept in doorways at night, mostly. There was lots of things to hide from there."

The Briarlane children regarded Arthur with awe. He slept in doorways in that big, noisy city?

"What did you eat?" Bert asked.

"Anything we could find. Lots of restaurants threw

things out in the alley, and we picked food up. Sometimes we snitched fruit from the stands."

"You mean you took it when they weren't looking?"

Arthur could see that this wasn't a good thing to talk about. "Well, sometimes the owners would give us what was left over at the end of the day. We didn't snitch a whole lot."

"The folks at Hull House were good to us," Trudy put in. "They took in all the kids they could there. Nobody else ever gave us brand-new clothes before."

"That's why we believed 'em when they said we'd get new homes out here, and people would want us," Nell added.

"We're going to see who wants us this time," Shala declared as the train lurched to a stop. The children turned again to the windows and gazed at the crowd who lined the platform. There were farmers in overalls and straw hats. Some businessmen in fine suits stood among them. Sunbonnets and apron-covered cotton dresses mingled with the latest fashions in gowns, and feathered and beribboned hats.

"Stay right here until I come back for you," Charles Glover instructed them. "I'll make arrangements with the town folk and find out where we are to go."

"Do you see someone you'd like to go home with?" Alice whispered to Betsy.

"There's a lady who's smiling and waving," Betsy said. "She looks nice. But I think I'd rather stay with you. I'd like us to go to the same town."

Alice nodded. "I'd like all of us to go to the same place. Even Philip."

"Philip always teases you. Why would you want him?"

" 'Cause I know him," Alice replied. "I feel better with people I know even if I don't like them very much."

Betsy seemed to understand this, and the girls continued to watch the people outside.

At another window, Ethan and Bert were doing the same.

"They're going at this backwards," Bert observed. "Us kids need to pick the ma and pa we'd like 'stead of them picking us. I can tell from here that he doesn't like boys." Bert pointed toward a tall, thin man dressed in a black suit, a white shirt, and a string tie.

Ethan studied the man closely. "How do you know that?" he asked finally. "He looks all right to me."

"He's standing too quiet. And he's not talking to nobody. He looks like he was here to pick up a load of furniture. A chair won't talk back to him, but a boy will. He won't like that."

Ethan surveyed the crowd on the platform. It was true that most everyone was chatting with a neighbor or walking back and forth past the windows. They seemed excited and interested. Ethan looked back at the tall, unsmiling man standing alone.

"He doesn't look very happy, does he? Maybe he wants a child to cheer him up. Maybe living alone makes you look like that."

"It'd take a carload of kids to cheer him up," Bert said. "I don't want to be one of 'em."

"Pretend you could have anyone out there you wanted for your folks," Ethan said. "Who would you pick?"

Bert looked carefully, then shook his head. "They ain't

out there. My ma had soft, curly hair around her face. Theirs is all pulled back tight. My pa would be dancin' a jig to make folks laugh. I don't see 'em."

"You mean you're looking for your real folks?" Ethan stared at Bert. "You know they never lived in Iowa!"

Bert grinned sheepishly. "Naw, I ain't looking for 'em really. I'd just like new ones that looked like 'em. That way, see, I wouldn't have to get used to two different sets when my pa and ma do come back. 'Cause I'll find 'em when I'm sixteen and can go looking. Just wait and see."

Ethan had the feeling that even Bert didn't believe that, but he knew his friend wanted to, so he didn't argue.

"Sure you will, Bert. Maybe I'll even be able to help you look."

"Mr. Glover's coming back," someone said. "Are we going now?"

Simon climbed up on the seat where Ethan stood at the window. "She's here, too," he announced.

"Who's here, Simon?"

"That little bitty lady I didn't smack in the nose."

Ethan opened his mouth to tell Simon not to be ridiculous, but he had no chance. Mr. Glover was speaking.

"We're ready, children. Small ones with Matron, the rest line up by size and follow me. The people are anxious to see you."

New shoes squeaked down the train aisle and descended the big, metal steps. The crowd parted to make way for this unusual parade, and it seemed like hundreds of eyes followed as they headed toward the church a short distance away.

5

LIBERTY

I hear a train coming, Mama! Is it the Orphan Train?"

"I expect so, dear." The woman adjusted the white straw hat that bounced off the little girl's head and hung around her neck by the elastic.

"Do stop dancing around, Glory. Your clothes will be a mess. You'll look just like an orphan."

"Really, Harriet, that was hardly the best choice of words." The woman beside her reproved her sister sharply. "The child will think that the boy you take will have to look like a tramp."

Harriet Hodge glanced around at her neighbors. "I know, Edna. It just slipped out. But you don't ever expect an orphan to look neat and tidy, do you?"

"I think you'll have to tell me again why you've decided to take one." Edna sighed and looked down the track toward the approaching train. "It seems a most foolhardy thing to do."

"Glory wants a playmate. I can't think of an easier way than this to get one. Frank didn't object. He thought it might be nice to have a boy to take into the business."

"At seven years of age?"

"No, of course not. If we get one we like, we intend to keep him."

"And if you don't like him?"

"We can always send him back."

"You make the child sound like a piece of merchandise. Are you sure Frank won't sell him if he gets tired of him?"

"Oh, for goodness' sakes, Edna! Be sensible. You know better than that."

Edna's face said that she didn't, but she made no further comment. Harriet turned her attention to the little girl.

"Glory, why are you pulling on my skirt? I'm going to look as bedraggled as you do before that train ever gets here. What do you want?"

"I'm going to pick him out, huh, Mama?"

"Oh, I suppose so," her mother replied. "Just don't grab the first one you see getting off the train. Remember that he's going to live in the same house with us."

Edna watched the people standing along the boardwalk in front of the depot. Some, she knew, had come out of curiosity, as she had herself. But many others were planning to return home with one of these children. It would certainly be interesting to know what all their reasons were.

The small town of Liberty lay along the Iowa River, less

than one hundred miles from Davenport. Not many strangers came through; none who were unobserved. There had been great excitement when the notice of the Orphan Train appeared on the post office door and on Hodge's mercantile window. Since everyone in town and many in the surrounding countryside entered those two establishments daily, there was no one who was unaware of the great event.

"I didn't even know I wanted another young one until I saw that notice," Mrs. Tyler declared. "Just imagine being able to pick whoever you want from the bunch. I'm going to get a girl who can cook and sew. I just hate to cook and sew."

"You're not too fond of mopping and washing clothes, either," her daughter, Nita, observed. "You'd better be sure the girl can do that, too."

The mother ignored the girl and turned to the woman next to her. "How about you, Jenna? What are you getting?"

"I don't know yet. We want to look them over and choose a child who looks needy. Of course, they're all needy," she added quickly, "but I think I'll know the one for us when I see them all together. Jared and I want a child we can love and bring up to serve the Lord."

"Well, I suppose there isn't that much work to do in a parsonage," Mrs. Tyler replied. "Your husband only works on Sunday, and the church folks support you. I guess you do have a garden though, don't you?"

Jenna smiled and answered quietly. "Yes, we have a

garden. I hope our child will enjoy working in the earth, but the chores will be handed out evenly among us, just as they are now. I'm not planning to adopt a servant."

Mrs. Tyler blushed and turned away. The minister's wife had obviously heard Nita's remarks. Her daughter needed some competition, Mrs. Tyler thought irritably. She was far too free to speak her mind.

Clayton Jones stood by himself, staring thoughtfully down the track. There might not have been anyone else on the platform for all the notice he gave them. Since reading the advertisement in the *Iowa County Courier* several weeks ago, Clayton had thought of little else. He had briefly discussed the matter with his sister, who shared his home.

"You know it will be all right with me, Clayton. I'd a little prefer that you'd get a wife first, but that's up to you. I'm happy to stay right here and look after you and the boy."

"Thank you, Cassie. You've been patient over the years. Unfortunately they are not sending Suitable Wife Trains to Iowa this season. It is becoming a matter of necessity that I have help in the business, and I want it to stay in the family. I'm unsure how to approach a boy with the possibilities ahead for him."

Cassie nodded. *Well you might be*, she thought. *If you're looking for an apprentice, he's not going to have years to grow used to the situation.* She tried to envision the child's reaction when he viewed the sign "Jones and Son" over the local funeral parlor.

Clayton had much the same misgiving. It had been four years now since his beloved wife and only son had fallen victim to the smallpox epidemic that swept the area. Clayton had thought to carry on alone, but as he grew older, he realized that not only did he need help in his work, he needed a family of his own.

The thought that his occupation could be objectionable to some boys had entered his head, but his greater concern was about knowing what to do with a boy of fourteen or fifteen. He supposed they would need to carry on a conversation occasionally, but he had no idea what boys wanted to talk about. The few that he had observed about town seemed to lean strongly toward things like, "Hey, Spike! Whatcha doin'?" or "Sez your old man!" and things equally unintelligible. City children would probably come equipped with a vocabulary completely foreign to him.

As the train drew closer, Clayton's apprehension grew stronger. Should he turn and go back home? Should he just go ahead and apprentice the Wilcox boy, whose father had an eye on eventually owning the entire main street where Clayton's acre occupied a choice spot? The thought of the elder Wilcox's continual pushing of such an alliance strengthened Clayton's resolve, and he stood his ground.

No one walking by the tall, somber man clad in a black suit, white shirt, and black string tie would ever suspect that he was pondering anything but death.

Among those milling about the platform, anxiously

awaiting the arrival of the children, was Julia Thornton. She had come many miles since morning to meet this train. The conversation with her husband Isaac the evening before remained fresh in her mind.

"Be heading for summer pasture next week," Isaac said.

Julia rocked in silence for several minutes, then spoke in her soft voice. "I'm not staying here alone this summer, Isaac."

Her husband stared as though he had never seen her before. "Where you staying then?"

"I said I won't be staying here alone. I'm going to Liberty tomorrow and get me an orphan from the train. I made arrangements when I first read the ad last month."

"You never needed no company any other year." Isaac was puzzled. "You going to get an orphan to spend the summer? What are you going to do with him then? You never minded being here alone before."

"Her. I've hated being here alone. It's all I could do not to pack up the milk cows and the chickens and follow you up there. And I'm not getting an orphan for the summer. She'll stay here for good. Do you know how long it's been since I've had any womenfolk to talk to? I want a girl I can teach to cook and make dresses for and play tea party with. I want somebody who looks like me with long hair to brush and ribbons to tie. I might get two of them. I'm tired of being the only woman within fifty miles of this place. Not to mention the only human for four months of the year while you're gone."

Isaac had been shocked into total silence, Julia

remembered. He had eyed her cautiously this morning, but the buggy was standing ready when she emerged at dawn in a clean, crisply starched cotton dress and bonnet.

"There's food aplenty for you and the boys," she said as she took up the reins. "I'll stay at Sadie's tonight and be back tomorrow afternoon."

Isaac nodded and stepped back as the buggy rolled out the lane.

" 'Fraid yer ma's gone past it," he muttered to the tall son who stood beside him. "We'd best get at the chores."

Now as Julia watched the smoke billow from the engine approaching them, her appearance did not indicate that she had "gone past it." Her eyes sparkled, and she smiled at everyone who walked by. Her cousin Sadie, delighted to have an overnight visitor, was nevertheless at a loss to explain Julia's behavior.

"I don't understand, Julia. You're fifty-eight years old and you have seven boys. Why in the world do you want to take on another young one at your age? If you need more help around the place you could get a hired girl."

"Mercy, no. I don't need help. Not for taking care of the house and garden, anyway. What I need is company. I want someone who speaks the same language I do."

"I'd of thought those boys of yours would be married by now and you'd have some girls. How old's the youngest one?"

"Eighteen this summer. They're all busy with the ranch, and that's all they think about. At least the four oldest have houses of their own in case they want to find a wife. I guess

no girl wants to live that far from civilization." Julia paused
and reflected on the endless miles of pasture over which
Isaac ran his cattle. As much as she had desired daughters-
in-law, she had to admit that the prospects were pretty
bleak. She needed to take steps to remedy things herself.
That's why she was here.

"What age girl you looking to get?" Sadie was asking.
"And where you going to send her to school?"

Julia had thought about that.

"I don't care what age she is. Or they are. I'm thinking
of two girls. They'll be company for each other. But
schooling will have to be done at home. I was a teacher
before I married Isaac, you know. I taught all the boys to
read and write and cipher. I inherited Pa's library and Ma's
organ. We'll get on fine with education. I just don't want
them to be lonesome."

"What does Isaac think about this?" Sadie wanted to know.

"Isaac?" Julia seemed surprised at the question. "Why,
he never said. He leaves things like that up to me. 'Tain't as
if I was buying him a new herd of cattle, you know."

The ladies turned their attention to the train which was
puffing to a stop, and waited expectantly for the doors to open.

Caleb Pritchard, Liberty's only attorney and mayor of
the town, also waited for the appearance of Charles Glover,
the agent for the placement program. He was glad that his
wife, Electra, had chosen not to be on hand this afternoon.
She had strongly disapproved of the whole idea.

"Look at this list of people who want to adopt children," she said. "How could you possibly recommend all of them? There aren't more than five families on here who would be fit to raise a child!"

Caleb couldn't deny that. "I've tried to look at both sides of the question. I can't be the judge of anyone's motives. All I know is that most any child has a better chance of survival in a home, with family, than he has on a city street, eating out of garbage cans."

"I'd rather eat out of garbage cans than live with Cora Tyler, I can tell you that," his wife declared.

Caleb silently agreed, but he felt an obligation to defend his role in the matter.

"It's not as though it has to be a permanent arrangement if it doesn't work out," he said. "If a child doesn't adjust, he can be removed and placed elsewhere."

"Well, I'm glad I'm not one to be chosen today to be moved around like a pawn on a chess board. It's hard enough to grow up in the family you're born into."

Caleb pondered this philosophy as he paced the station platform. He was living proof that this was so. His father, Judge Pritchard, had insisted on his firstborn son following in his footsteps.

"There's always been a Pritchard in law," he'd said. "Don't take it into your head to think that you'll do any differently. A blacksmith indeed! Use your common sense, boy. You'll be a lawyer."

In spite of the success of his career, Caleb still resented being pushed into his father's choice. Electra was right—it was not easy to grow up. He was still being pushed, Caleb admitted. The list his wife had read was folded in his pocket, but he didn't need to look at it to know who was included.

John Muller shouldn't have been approved for a child, but Caleb felt he had no choice. His position as mayor depended upon the goodwill of John Muller. If Caleb had turned the man down because of the harsh treatment he gave his own family, there would soon be another mayor. Ernest Rubeck wanted another farmhand and would probably not send the boy to school as required, but he held the note on Caleb's house. The Sinclairs were too old to raise a child, but they were fellow church members. How could he explain cutting them from the list?

Caleb stopped and wiped his brow with a big handkerchief. What his neighbors did wasn't his responsibility, he reasoned. At any rate, the train had stopped and agent Glover was coming toward him. Caleb pushed his weary thoughts away and met Charles with a big smile and a hardy handshake.

6

THE CHOSEN ONES

Ethan watched the boys and girls line up across the platform of the church. Matron had told everyone to smile at the people when they came in, but even Louis, who was the most cheerful boy Ethan knew, had a terrible scowl on his face.

"I guess I wouldn't feel like smiling if I was up there," Ethan said to Matron. "I'm glad I'm sitting down here by you."

Matron patted his knee. "They are frightened right now, I'm sure. It will be better when the folks begin to talk to them."

From the other side of Matron, Alice leaned around to speak to her brother. "I'm going to miss Betsy something awful. Are you going to miss Bert?"

Ethan didn't look at Alice. "Yeah. But maybe no one will take them today."

Matron Daly's heart ached for the children as she listened to them sing and recite for the strangers. She hugged Will, who sat on her lap, and glanced at Simon. He had chosen to sit on the end of a front pew to watch the activity with wide-open eyes. He'd begged to sing with the others, but they couldn't run the risk of someone choosing him and being disappointed because Simon wasn't available.

Matron and Charles Glover had talked about how difficult this time would be.

"I worry about the ones like Arthur," Matron said. "How will a boy who has not spent a day in school feel about being confined in a building? He'll be laughed at and teased because he can't read or write. Will he be able to live like that?"

"It is hard," Charles agreed. "I trust each one of these children to the Lord as I let them go. I've found that most of the older boys do very well when they find that someone is willing to teach them a trade and treat them as a family member. We have to remember, Matron, that these children are survivors. If they couldn't make it almost anywhere, they wouldn't be here today."

Now the little program was over, and Ethan listened to the people around him talking about his friends.

"Mercy! I hope those children can do other things better than they sing!" This comment came from Cora Tyler.

Her daughter Nita yawned. "I'm sure you don't have to carry a tune to be able to scrub a floor. Just look for a strong girl who seems to be halfway intelligent."

"That tall girl on the end might be all right," Mrs. Tyler decided.

"That's Shala!" Ethan whispered to Matron. "The lady won't want her!"

Matron Daly nodded and smiled to herself. Ethan was right. This woman might get more intelligence than she could deal with if she took Shala. Here was one girl who would not be a slave for anyone.

The good people of Liberty began to walk past the rows of children, ready to select a new member for their families. Cora Tyler approached the end of the line with determination. She stopped before Shala and stared at the name tag fastened to the girl's white pinafore.

Pointing her finger in that direction, she demanded, "What kind of a name is that?"

Shala's mouth dropped open in surprise, then little sparks of fire appeared in her eyes.

"It's Irish, ma'am. I'm Shala O'Brien."

"Ridiculous name. But we can always change that. I suppose you know how to cook and clean, don't you? Can you sew?"

Shala smiled brightly, and Matron, watching her, knew that Mrs. Tyler had reason to beware.

"Oh, yes, ma'am. I'm a wonderful worker. I'm very quick, and I never do a job halfway. You wouldn't have any reason to complain about me. I can do anything you ask."

Mrs. Tyler was looking more pleased by the moment.

"Well. This sounds just fine, doesn't it, Nita? We'll take you. Come along, Sha—whatever your name is."

Shala bobbed a little curtsy. "Thank you, ma'am, but I would like to know if you pay by the day or by the job. Do most ladies of Liberty hire a girl, so I'll have lots of work?"

This time it was Cora Tyler's mouth that dropped open.

"Pay? Who said anything about pay? I'm going to adopt you!"

Shala managed to look disappointed. "You are? I thought you wanted me to come and work for you. I'm old enough to hire out, and I'm saving to go to normal school and be a teacher. I probably won't do, will I?"

Nita laughed out loud at her mother's obvious discomfort. "I guess you've met your match this time, Mama. I think you should take her. We'd get along fine."

Cora Tyler glared at her daughter and marched toward the door. "Cheeky girl," she muttered. "Just what you'd expect of an orphan."

Ethan watched in puzzlement as Matron suddenly bent over to retie Will's shoes, and Caleb Pritchard was forced to leave for water to ease a coughing fit. Wasn't anyone going to speak to Shala about being sassy? Sometimes it was hard to understand grown folks.

He turned his attention to the boys and girls lined up in front of him. Little Ruby, who came from Chicago, had grown weary. Now she sat down on the edge of the platform with one foot placed on top of the other and her chin resting on her knees. With her arms wrapped around her legs, she appeared to be almost asleep. Ethan noticed however, that her eyes were wide open, and Ruby didn't miss anything that was happening.

The people who walked by glanced at the top of her head, then went on. Ethan was about to point this out to Matron when the Rev. Jared Burke and his wife, Jenna, sat down on either side of the little girl. Ruby's head came up, and she looked at them anxiously.

"Hello. What's your name?"

Ruby sat up straight and revealed her name tag.

"Ruby. What a lovely name! Do you know that a ruby is something precious?"

The child shook her head and watched Jared carefully.

"We're looking for someone precious to take home with us. Would you like to be the one?"

For the first time the little girl spoke. "Really?"

"Really. Are you all by yourself?"

"No. There's Pete."

"Is Pete your brother?"

She nodded and pointed to the ten year old who stood with the boys. He was watching his little sister. When Jenna arose and walked toward him, Pete stiffened and stood as straight as he could. His face was pale, but he met Jenna's gaze directly.

"Hello, Pete."

"Hello, ma'am." He studied her carefully. "Be you goin' to take my little sister?"

"We'd like to. Would that be all right with you?"

Pete nodded. "Yes, ma'am. You look kind. She's a good girl, but she don't know much about living in a house. We ain't had one lately."

"How old are you, Pete?"

"Ten. 'Most eleven, I think."

He doesn't look any older than the girl, Jenna thought. *They both need some good food.* She smiled at him.

"Would you like to come with Ruby and live with us?"

Pete looked around as though he wasn't sure she had spoken to him.

"Me? You want me, too?"

"We certainly do." She took his hand. "Come and meet your new papa."

Ethan looked on with pleasure as the Burkes each took a child and went to talk with Agent Glover. When they left the church together a few minutes later, he noticed that Matron was brushing a tear from her eye.

Suddenly Ethan's attention was drawn to a disturbance at the front of the church. A girl had grabbed Simon's arm and was attempting to pull him to his feet. Simon was clinging desperately to the pew. As Ethan raced to the rescue, the girl shouted, "This one's mine!"

Ethan snatched Simon and jerked him back. "You can't have him. He's already been adopted."

"I don't see anyone coming to get him." Glory Hodge looked around the room. "Mama said I could have any one I wanted, and I want him."

"Well, that's too bad, because you can't have him. He's my brother and he goes with me."

"Mama!" Glory screamed and stamped her foot. "Tell this horrid boy that his brother is mine. Make him turn him loose!"

Both Mrs. Hodge and Charles Glover ran to the scene.

"Of course you shall have him, Glory. What is the problem here, young man?" She glared at Ethan and took hold of Simon's shoulder.

"I'm sorry, ma'am," Charles broke in. "Ethan is right. Simon isn't available for adoption."

"What's he doing up here then?" Harriet Hodge's fancy hat shook with indignation. "These are all orphans, aren't they? I should think we could have the one we want."

Charles thought quickly. "Yes, ma'am. You may have your choice, but if you take this one, you must also take his two brothers and sister. They stay together as a family."

Mrs. Hodge backed away with a gasp. "Four children? Well, I never!"

"We make it a policy not to separate siblings from each other unless it is absolutely necessary. Someone has offered to take these four."

"Well, I never. Come along, Glory. You'll just have to play with the children at school."

Glory stamped her foot again. "But, Mama, you promised!"

"I'm not going to adopt a whole orphanage, even for you," Harriet told her. "Come along."

She swept out of the church with a protesting Glory in tow. A pleased sister Edna followed them, nodding to her neighbors as she passed.

Charles mopped his forehead and escorted the boys back to Matron. Ethan was visibly shaken, but Simon had other concerns.

"I wish people would stop pulling my arms," he said.

As the afternoon wore on, several other children were spoken for. Three-year-old Millie went with a young couple. Martin, aged twelve, was taken by a kindly looking farmer and his wife. The schoolmaster from a neighboring town chose six-year-old Duane, because, he said to Charles, "The boy has my red hair and my father's name! How could we leave him here?"

"It looks like Billy picked his own folks," Ethan observed. "He's still hanging on to that man."

Matron smiled at the picture they were watching. The small boy clung to the farmer's pants leg as the man talked with his wife.

"It's up to you," the woman told him. "He's already decided that he's going with you. You'll have to pry him loose if you don't take him."

The man leaned over and took Billy in his arms. There was no question about the outcome. Billy had found a home and a family, and he wasn't going to let them get away.

Will had fallen asleep on Matron's lap, so she was content to continue watching the activities around her. Of special interest was the tall, thin man who stood apart from the others, apparently just observing, although he nodded and spoke to his neighbors when they looked at him. He had studied each child so carefully that Matron was curious as to what he might be thinking.

Ethan had been watching him, too. This was the man that didn't like boys, according to Bert. Ethan wasn't so sure about that. Close up, the man looked sad and worried, but not mean.

"A lot of people are gone," Ethan said to Matron. "Can I go and sit by Bert for a while?"

"I don't know why not," Matron replied. "Be quiet and don't run around. I think we'll be going back to the train before long."

"Lots of folks found kids today," Bert remarked. "I still haven't seen anyone I wanted to take me. Especially not that one."

As though he had heard Bert's statement, Clayton Jones started toward the front of the church.

"Uh oh." Bert looked worried.

"Maybe he wants a girl," Ethan whispered.

Apparently he did not, for Clayton headed for the boys and stopped in front of Arthur. From where they sat, Bert and Ethan could hear the conversation.

"Well, young man, how old are you?"

"Fourteen, sir." Arthur straightened his shoulders and looked the man in the eye. "I'm strong and I ain't afraid to work."

"I need a boy to go into business with me," Clayton told him. "You would be apprenticed until you are sixteen, then if you do well and wish to do so, you may become a partner."

Arthur's eyes sparkled. "Really, sir? I ain't had no schooling, but I can do whatever you show me. What kind of business have you got?"

"I'm a mortician."

This was met with a blank look from Arthur. "A mortician?"

"Yes. I arrange for all the funerals in this part of the country."

Arthur's face cleared. "Oh, you takes care of stiffs. I know about that. I seen as many dead folks as I have live ones. You just tell me what to do."

Mr. Jones cleared his throat. "I must tell you that I have never had a boy your age, and I may need some help in learning how to treat a son."

"Oh, that's nothing," Arthur assured him. "I ain't never had a pa neither. We can start out together." He looked around the room. "I think I can put a little grub on the table if there ain't no ma at home."

"That sounds wonderful," Clayton told him, "but it won't be necessary. My sister will take care of us very well. I know she is going to like you—as well as I do."

Arthur came over and poked Riley on the arm. "I got me a home, Rile," he said joyfully. "This here's my new pa. Matron was giving it to us straight. You just wait—you'll get one."

Bert and Ethan watched in silence as Arthur and Clayton Jones walked out of the church together.

"Now that's what I'm waiting for," Bert said finally.

"I don't think he's going to dance a jig on the platform," Ethan returned.

"That's all right. I just want a pa that fits. That one fits Arthur."

The day had almost ended, and still the two little ladies

in starched cotton dresses and bonnets sat quietly on the front pew of the church.

"Don't you think you should go and claim the girls you want before they're all taken?"

"No, I don't think so, Sadie," Julia Thornton replied. "The ones the Lord wants me to have will be there when the crowd is gone. I'll wait. A few more minutes won't be anything after waiting forty years."

"I s'pose so. But have you seen some that take your eye?"

"Well, yes, but I won't set my heart on them. All these poor little young ones need someone to love them. I'll be happy with any girl there."

At that moment, Betsy looked up at Julia and smiled at her. Julia beckoned to the little girl, and Betsy came to stand in front of her.

"I saw you smiling and waving when we were on the train," Betsy said to her. "I told Alice that I'd like you. Alice can't stay here," she added sadly. "She has to go with her brothers. Wouldn't it be nice to have brothers?"

Julia laughed happily. "How would you like to have seven of them?"

Betsy's eyes widened. "Seven?"

"That's how many you'll have if you come home with me," Julia replied. "They'll all look after you and your little sister."

"I don't have a sister, ma'am. There's just me. Does that mean you don't want me?"

"Oh, my, no! That means we'll choose another little girl. Can you help me pick one?"

"I've been helping to take care of Kate," Betsy said. "I like her a lot."

"Then let's talk to Mr. Glover, shall we?"

While it was being arranged with the agent, Alice and Betsy hugged each other and cried.

"That's how I'll feel when you get adopted," Ethan told Bert. "But I probably won't cry. I don't think boys do that."

"They do on the inside," Bert said. "I know I will."

"All right, boys and girls," Matron called. "It's time to go back to our cars. We'll have our supper and go to bed early. This has been a long day."

Sixteen weary children trudged back to the Orphan Train, Ethan and Bert dragging a sleepy Simon between them.

"We'll miss ol' Arthur," Bert said. "I don't think the man looked quite so sad when they left. Arthur was just what he needed to cheer him up."

Supper was simple and quick, and before the sky was fully darkened, every child was rolled up in his blanket for the night. No one stirred when the next train west backed into the siding, coupled on the Orphan Train and the three cars behind it, and chugged noisily away from Liberty.

7

SIMON'S
ADVENTURE

Whenever the train stopped at a station, Simon didn't rush to the windows with the others to watch the people milling about the platform. Instead, he found a place by the window on the other side of the coach. This, he had found, was where the exciting things were happening. No one else had discovered it yet. It wasn't that Simon was deliberately keeping it to himself. He had tried to tell Ethan and Bert.

"I saw her again. She's still here."

"Simon, are you talking about the lady in Davenport?" Ethan was becoming impatient. "It's all right to tell make-believe stories, but you have to know when they aren't true."

"It is true. She has on a little hat, and she carries a purse."

"If you see her every day, how come the rest of us don't?" Bert asked. "You'd think someone else would catch sight of her."

" 'Cause you look out the wrong window. There's other people, too. And big bunches of hay, and. . . ."

Ethan shook his arm. "Simon, I'll have to get Matron to talk to you if you keep on telling stories like that. Now cut it out!"

If no one was going to believe him, Simon decided, he would have to prove it to them. How he could do this, he didn't know. Ethan and Bert kept an eye on him every minute when they left the train. Sometimes they had only ten or fifteen minutes outdoors at a stop. It wasn't long enough for Simon to find a way to the other side of the tracks.

His chance came when Mr. Glover announced, "We'll be at Cedar Rapids for quite a while this morning. Our cars will sit on the siding while they add new coaches and another engine. You may all go out and watch, but stay clear of the tracks. We'll be in the same place on the train, so look for the scarf on the door bar."

Everyone stayed close together and watched with excitement as the train backed onto a rail close to the station. The noise was deafening as yard workers shouted to each other and couplings were undone. Cars banged and jumped apart. The engine, the coal car, the freight and mail cars went forward. Whistles blew and steam puffed around as they reversed directions and ended on an outside rail.

"Wow! Did you see that? The engineer knew just where to back up! I can see the cars up there that they're going to hitch up to." With Simon between them, Ethan and Bert raced down the platform to watch.

Simon's feet could not go that fast. When he stumbled

and fell to his knees, he'd had enough. "I'm tired of being pulled around," he complained. "I'll wait here until you come back."

Ethan knew he shouldn't go on without Simon, but he did want to watch the changing of the cars. He was sure that Simon wouldn't leave the platform, and they would be straight back to get him.

"Well, all right. But don't you dare move from this spot. We'll be up there." Ethan pointed to the engine just ahead of them. "I can still see you, so don't try to go somewhere else."

Simon nodded and stood with his back against the station house. Bert and Ethan went on, leaving the little boy to watch the train and people walking in and out of the depot. He could see the engine up ahead backing into another track. The gap between it and their cars had widened considerably, and Simon moved closer to the track to look through. The view wasn't as good as it had been from the window. Since nothing stood in the way, perhaps he could run to the other side and back before Ethan returned. Looking toward the engine, Simon saw that both Bert and Ethan were watching the new cars being picked up and weren't paying attention to him. Quickly he dashed across the tracks and disappeared behind the coaches of the Orphan Train.

"Hey, look!" Bert shouted over the noise. "All those cars are waiting to be fastened on. Then they'll back up and hitch ours on again. How do you s'pose the engineer can see all that from up there?"

Riley was standing behind them. "They have switchmen to take care of that," he explained. "See them?" He pointed to several men who were pulling giant levers and moving sections of the track. The boys watched in fascination as the new cars were added, the engine switched back to the original track, and then the whole thing was backed up to be coupled again to the Orphan Train.

"Come on, boys," Riley said. "We'll be leaving in a few minutes. We'd better head back to our coach." He looked around quickly. "Where's Simon?"

"We left him at the station house. He's standing there watching the train. See?" Ethan's heart sank as he turned toward the depot. Simon was not there.

"Maybe he just went inside for a minute," Bert suggested.

"Or maybe he went around back to get a drink, like we did the other time," Ethan said. "He has to be there somewhere."

A frantic look in both directions revealed no Simon.

"We'll have to get Mr. Glover." Bert pulled Ethan toward the car with the scarf tied to it. The *whoo, whoo* of the train whistle told them that they would have to hurry.

"Don't worry," Riley said. "I'm sure someone took Simon back to our car. Matron and Mr. Glover always look around the platform and count us before the train leaves. Hurry and get on."

Charles Glover ran up behind them. "Good. There you

are. I was afraid I'd have to ask the conductor to have them wait for you." He ushered them into the first car where the others had already gathered. Matron counted and as she got to "fifteen," the train began to move.

"Fifteen? I must have counted wrong." She started to count again. Charles moved down the swaying aisle and numbered them out loud. "One, two, three . . . fifteen! Who's missing?"

"Simon," Riley said. "We thought he was already on."

Ethan, near tears, was pressed against the window watching the rapidly disappearing platform fade behind them.

"He must be," Charles said. "I'd have seen him out there. He's probably gone into the other car."

A thorough search of the coach revealed no little boy. Charles came back and sat down to decide what to do next. He studied the schedule carefully. "I'll have to get off at the next stop and find a way back to Cedar Rapids," he decided. "We're going west now instead of north, and the next town for coal and water is Ames. We won't be there until morning."

"What will happen to Simon?" Ethan was trying not to cry, but tears ran down his cheeks.

Matron put her arm around him. "Don't worry, Ethan. The station manager won't let a little boy stand around alone. He'll look after Simon until Mr. Glover can get back there. We know that Simon didn't leave the train yard. He must have been behind the station and you just didn't see him."

"But he'll be scared. He's never been alone overnight!"

Matron sat down and pulled Ethan down beside her.

"Remember when Will disappeared from Briarlane, and I told you about the little lost lamb?"

Ethan nodded.

"We prayed," Matron continued, "and trusted the Lord to look after Will. You know that He did. Don't you think that the Good Shepherd can keep an eye on Simon, too?"

"I know that God can do that for Simon," Ethan confided in Bert a few minutes later, "but I wanted to keep my eye on him, too. I intended to watch, but we got so interested in the train, I forgot. Where would he go by himself?"

"I don't think he would go anywhere but the train," Bert said. "He might have climbed on another car."

Charles Glover had already considered that when they approached him with the possibility. He shook his head.

"I'm afraid not, boys. The cars ahead of us are all new ones that we picked up. The three behind us didn't open on the platform side of the train. There's no place where he could have gotten on alone."

It was a sober and dismal suppertime on the Orphan Train that evening. Even though Mr. Glover assured them that Simon would be safe and back with them the next day, the children were concerned about the little boy. No one wanted to think that he had been taken away from the station by anyone, but Ethan feared that he might have.

After the boys and girls were asleep, Charles and Matron discussed what would need to be done.

"I think we'd better arrange to stay on a siding in Ames until I get back," Charles decided. "There's no point in your going on to the next town alone, since I'm needed to make the arrangements for adoptions."

"I'd go back for him myself," Matron said, "but I'm not sure that Shala could handle the girls and the cooking."

"The children need you more than they do me," Charles replied. "I'll telegraph ahead and tell them we'll be a day late on our route. We're about halfway through Iowa when we get to Ames."

So the matter was left, and Agent Glover dozed restlessly as he waited for morning. It was earlier than his usual rising time when he folded his blanket and prepared for the stop. The car was dark as he made his way to the washroom and readied himself for the day. On the way back to his place, as was his habit, Charles glanced at each boy as he passed the seats where they lay. Automatically he counted as he looked. "One, two, three . . . ten."

Ten! There were only nine boys last night! Quickly he went back down the aisle, peering closely at each child in the dim light. Curled up in the corner of one seat with no blanket around him was Simon.

After Simon had scooted across the tracks to the other side of the train, he'd been disappointed to see nothing but rails over there. This was where he had always seen the little lady and others walking. This was where a wagon with bales of hay had come up beside the cars that were being pulled behind the Orphan Train. Where were they now?

As he looked around with uncertainty, Simon spied something unusual. Instead of the solid wooden boxcars that he had seen from the other side of the tracks, there were small slats of wood on this side. He walked over closer to get a better look. Little wisps of hay stuck out between the slats, and Simon could hear thumping and stamping and stomping. Was this a barn on wheels? It certainly looked—and smelled—like one, he thought. The cracks were not far enough apart so that he could see through to the dark interior. As he walked the length of the two cars, strange noises reached him. They didn't sound like the animals he was used to hearing, but what else could they be?

Simon was used to the racket of the train cars banging, whistles blowing, and men shouting. The steam rising from the wheels, the soot falling from the smokestack, and the cinders skittering along the rails were not new either. So he didn't notice when the engine and coaches were backed up and coupled to the Orphan Train cars. He did realize, though, that he'd better get back to the station house before Ethan missed him. He would be in trouble for moving away from that spot.

Running back to the other end of the boxcars, Simon was surprised to see that there was no empty space where he had crossed the tracks. The two cars that he thought were theirs stood in place, but now there were many others in front of them. Simon looked between the cars and saw the station on the other side. There was no way to get to it, unless he crawled over the coupling. This, he decided, would not be easy. He would try to get around the end of the train.

By the time Simon had reached the last car on the train, he heard the familiar blast of steam and the *whoo*, *whoo* that meant that the train was about to leave. He didn't dare cross the tracks if those huge cars were moving. He stood still and stared up at the windows of the passenger coach, his heart thumping wildly.

Miss Carmen sat on the station side of the last coach on the train. As she looked idly out at the people hurrying by, she was hardly aware that her head barely rose above the windowsill, or that her feet swung high above the floor. She had never been much more than three feet tall, and she had become used to the fact that ordinary furniture hadn't been built with her in mind.

"I'll certainly be glad when we get to Ames," she said to the small person next to her. "I don't know why we had to go so far north of Davenport to be able to switch and go back to Des Moines."

"I'd say it's because that's the way they laid the tracks," her companion answered. "Looks on the map like Ames is the hub of Iowa. At least we didn't have to go too far west and backtrack."

"I guess that's right," Miss Carmen had to agree.

"We were so late leaving Florida this spring that we're fortunate to hitch on anywhere. This is the first time I've had to travel with the animal cars and the trainer."

Madame Mona nodded. "I know. It was too bad you were too ill to travel with the rest of the troupe. But you're better now, and this has been a comfortable trip. I'm glad they've let us get off on the opposite side of the coach. These little towns are swarming with people when we stop. What are they out there to see? Do they meet every train that way?"

"I don't think so," Carmen replied. "I think it must have something to do with those two cars ahead of us. They're loaded with children. Have you noticed them?"

"I thought I saw a lot of them running around up there, but it's hard to tell from back here. I never go out to walk on the platform side."

Across the aisle one of the animal trainers stood at the window. "You don't have to go outside to see them," he remarked. "There's one standing right under our windows."

Carmen and Mona both slid from their seats and hurried to the other side of the car.

"Why, that's the little boy I saw in Davenport!" Carmen exclaimed. "He's just a baby! What's he doing out there alone?"

As she spoke, they heard the *whoo, whoo* of the whistle for departure.

"Rudy! We can't leave that little boy out there! Go and get him!"

Rudy hesitated. "I can't do that, Carmen. What if he happens to be a kid who lives here in Cedar Rapids? They'd get me for kidnapping!"

"I tell you I saw him in Davenport," Carmen insisted. "He didn't get from there to here without being on this train. We're going to be moving in just a minute. You've got to go get him!"

As steam puffed around the wheels and smoke blew back from the engine, Rudy leaped down the steps, scooped Simon up under one arm, and bounded back into the car.

Charles gazed in disbelief at Simon, sleeping soundly in the seat across the aisle from Ethan. This was the place he usually occupied, but everyone knew that he had not been there the night before when the lights were extinguished. Where had he come from, and how had he gotten there?

Charles returned to his seat to ponder the situation. There would be no need to make arrangements for leaving the Orphan Train in Ames. Glancing at his watch, Charles saw that they would be arriving there within the hour. There was no need to awaken anyone yet.

It may not have been necessary, but in a very few minutes, it happened anyway. Bert awoke and saw Simon curled up on the seat.

"Hey, Ethan!" he shouted. "God brought him back! Simon's here!"

It didn't take long for the news to reach the girls' car, and soon everyone was gathered around the little boy, demanding to know what had happened. Simon's answers were brief and to the point.

"Where were you?"

"I was out there." Simon pointed out the window.

"How did you get back on here?"

"A man lifted me up."

"What man?"

"Rudy. He lives back there." Again Simon pointed, this time toward the back of the train.

"The little lady lives back there, too. She didn't have a hat on, but she gave me some supper. Then Rudy showed me some big animals on this train. El'phants and lions and tigers, and they made a lot of noise. Then Rudy opened our door and let me in here and I couldn't reach my blanket and I'm hungry."

Further questioning revealed nothing more about Simon's adventure. He had told all he knew, and with that they had to be satisfied.

THE BIG SHOW

Miss Carmen sat in the last coach on the train and looked back at herself from the reflection on the darkened window. Behind her she observed Madam Mona flipping through a magazine. Across the aisle, with their feet on the seats in front of them, sat Rudy and Jack, the animal trainers. There was nothing to be seen out the window, nor was much of interest going on inside the car. Finally Carmen turned and spoke to the others.

"I can't believe that child was out on the rails by himself," she said. "If you hadn't seen him, Rudy, he'd be out there yet, no doubt."

"Who'd have thought we had a whole load of orphans up ahead of us? There must be fifteen or twenty of 'em. I wonder where they're going."

"We don't know that they're all orphans," Mona said, "but I suppose if they have a matron taking care of them, they're not with a family. What are they going to do with that many children?"

No one had an answer to that, and they all sat, remembering the minutes after Simon was snatched up and brought into their car.

Rudy had placed the little boy on a seat, then sank down beside him. "Whew! We almost didn't make it! What were you doing out there, kid?"

Simon didn't answer. He was staring at Carmen and Mona, who stood in the aisle beside him. They weren't any taller than he was, and he was sitting down!

"What's your name?" Carmen asked.

"Simon."

"Were you riding on this train?"

Simon nodded.

"Are you with your folks?"

"Ain't got no folks. Some men came and carried Ma away, and I hid under the table. Ethan said that Ma went to heaven."

Mona clasped her hand over her mouth in horror. The poor child! "Then where's your pa?" she asked.

Simon struggled to remember what he had heard about that, but nothing was clear to him. He shrugged.

"I don't know. Gone."

"Well, what were you doing out there on those rails?" Carmen insisted.

"Looking for you."

"Looking for me? You don't even know me!"

"Ethan and Bert don't think I saw you. They said I made you up. I didn't mean to almost smack you in the nose. I didn't know your nose was down there."

"No, I suppose you didn't," Carmen said. "No harm done. But you have to be traveling with someone. They'll be looking for you. Who are you with?"

"Matron. And Ethan and Bert and Riley and Will and the girls and—"

"You were right," Mona said, turning to Carmen. "That car ahead of us is loaded with children. They can't all belong to one person."

"It sounds like they all might be orphans," Rudy offered. "But where are they going with them?"

"I'm hungry," Simon announced. "It's suppertime."

"You're right," Mona said. She reached into a bag and pulled out an apple. "Here, eat this, and I'll get Jack to fix you something hot. Do you like stew?"

Simon nodded and munched happily on the apple while he watched the activity in the car. He was soon fed a big bowl of meat and vegetables and a slice of bread with apple butter on it. This was followed by a generous piece of cake. Simon had not eaten like that since he'd left Briarlane.

"We can't keep him in here," Carmen said. "This matron must be frantic if she's missed him." She glanced out the window. "It's dark already. I hope no one stayed in Cedar Rapids to look for him."

"I'll take him up there," Rudy said. "I can tell the matron what happened."

"Maybe they'll let you come back and visit us before we leave Ames tomorrow," Carmen told Simon.

"Can I bring Ethan and Bert? Then they'll believe me."

"Sure you can. We'll be glad to see them."

"Come on, kid," Rudy said. "Let's go before it gets any later."

He took Simon's hand and led him toward the adjoining car.

"Better take a light," Jack suggested. "You have two cars to go through."

Rudy nodded and grabbed one of the lanterns that hung from the ceiling of the coach. The platform between the two cars swayed and creaked. Rudy pushed open the door on the other side and shoved Simon through ahead of him.

Cold air and the smell of animals hit them. Simon gasped, then turned around and buried his face in Rudy's pants leg.

Rudy looked down at him in surprise. "Oh. I forgot you didn't know what was in here. They're all in cages. They won't hurt you."

A sudden roar next to him caused Simon to hang on tighter. He didn't dare look to see where the noise had come from.

"All right. How about if I carry you?" Rudy set the lantern on the floor, reached down to lift Simon up in his arms, then stooped to retrieve the light. "There. Is that better?"

Simon put both arms around Rudy's neck and clung closer.

"Just don't shut off my air," Rudy told him. "Here, look. They won't get out. Don't you want to see all the animals?"

Simon lifted his head enough for one eye to peek out. "What is it?" he whispered.

"This one's a lion. Didn't you ever see one before?"

Simon shook his head, then became brave enough to

look around with both eyes. Rudy started slowly down the aisle between the barred cages.

"This one here is a tiger," he said. "He's a big cat."

Simon regarded the huge, striped animal with awe. It certainly didn't look like the cats he remembered at Briarlane. The long freight car was filled with "big cats" pacing the floors of their cages or stretched out on the straw, tails flipping back and forth.

"Wait until you see what's in the next car," Rudy told him. "I suppose you never saw an elephant, either. Now, they are really big."

This, Simon found, was certainly true. He had never seen any living thing that huge before. Not even the work-horses of the orphanage stood that tall. Suddenly one of the animals thrust its trunk between the bars, and Simon shrieked in terror.

"Whoa, whoa," Rudy reassured him. "She won't bite. This here's Priscilla. She just wants a handout."

Rudy put the lantern down again and dug in his overall pocket. Simon watched as Priscilla daintily took a handful of peanuts in her trunk and transferred them to her mouth.

"I don't suppose you'd like to give her some?"

Simon's head shook wildly.

"All right, then. Let's go on. Over here's a couple of babies."

Rudy held the light high, and Simon gazed at two small elephants lying in the straw. These babies were bigger than the hog he had encountered on the farm, bigger even than the cows he stayed away from in the barn. Simon was grateful for the safety of Rudy's arms, even though he was assured that none of the animals could get loose.

When they finally reached the familiar boys' car, Rudy set Simon down on the floor. It was dark and quiet, and when Simon climbed up onto the empty seat and lay down, his new friend turned and went back to his coach.

Back in his own car, Rudy was met with a barrage of questions.

"Were they glad to see him?"

"Did they want to know where you found him?"

"How many kids are up there?"

"Where are they going?"

"I don't know any more than you do," Rudy replied. "The car was dark, and everyone I saw was asleep. I just put the boy down and left him."

"Are you sure you left him in the right car, Rudy?" Carmen was anxious. "Were the other children in there?"

"Looked like kids to me. Grown-ups don't go to sleep this early, and no one was walking around. You know what? That little kid never saw a wild animal before! Never even saw a picture of one, I guess. Scared to death, he was." Rudy chuckled. "Wouldn't even feed Priscilla some peanuts. Guess he thought she'd eat him, too." He sat down and stretched his legs out.

Carmen spoke again. "We'll be in Ames in the morning. What time do we leave for Des Moines?"

Rudy pulled the schedule from his pocket. "Six p.m. We'll be there all day to take on feed and water. Got time to look over the town if you want to."

"No, we get too many stares when people see us outside the circus tent. I was thinking that maybe the children's car won't be leaving right away, either. Perhaps we could entertain them while we're waiting."

Mona was excited about the idea. "If Simon never saw an animal, it's a pretty sure thing that not many of them have ever seen a circus! I say let's do it."

"It wouldn't be a big three ringer," Rudy said, "but we could put on a few acts. We can't let the animals out, but I can prop up the side of the cars in back so they can see them. I'll wear my clown suit and makeup."

Everyone thought of something that could be done in the small space they would have available.

"We'll all dress up," Rudy declared. "We've got a tumbling act, a juggling act, and the dogs. Let's do it!"

With the excitement of finding Simon all right, everyone was awake much earlier than usual. Matron decided they might as well get breakfast over with. Since it was barely light, they had a long day ahead of them.

"We'll be in Ames until evening," Charles Glover told them. "I understand that the cars ahead of us are going on north and the ones behind us go south. We'll keep on west toward Nebraska."

"Miss Carmen said we can come and see her," Simon announced between bites of breakfast roll.

Everyone stopped eating to look at him.

"Who's Miss Carmen?"

"The little bitty lady with . . ."

". . . the hat and purse!" Ethan finished the sentence for him. "Simon, I told you to cut it out! Nobody's going to believe you saw anyone like that. I'm not even sure you saw all those animals, either."

"Did." Simon continued his breakfast calmly. "Rudy will tell you."

"We didn't see any Rudy, either," Bert reminded him.

"He had to get back here some way," Riley put in. "There wasn't anyplace to hide when we were all looking for him last night. He couldn't have made all that up."

"All right, children," Matron said. "We'll believe what Simon told us until we know otherwise. Now we must decide what we'll do today if we stay in town. We simply cannot have anyone else almost missing the train or getting lost. Mr. Glover will make plans for us."

"We'll stay on the train until we're switched to a siding," Charles said. "You can watch from the windows. I'm going to do some shopping, and when I get back, we'll see about going to a park in town, together. No one will go off by himself. Is that understood?"

Heads nodded, and Shala looked at the boys with disdain.

"The girls always stay together," she said. "You don't see us running off and getting lost. Some of us know that Matron doesn't need any more work than she already has."

"Thank you, Shala," Matron said, "but we don't need a sermon. I'm sure the boys will be more careful today. How about getting our dishes washed up before the cars start banging back and forth?"

By the time the train stopped at Ames, everyone was ready for the day. This time the children gathered around the windows on the back of the car where Simon stood. "Just in case he really did see something we haven't seen," Bert said. Thus no one observed the tall man who stopped Charles Glover as he stepped from the train. No one could have heard their voices anyway, as Rudy made arrangements for the group to attend the afternoon's entertainment.

When the noon meal was ended, Matron gave directions for leaving the car. "Everyone walk with your partner. Simon will go with me this time, and Will can stay with Mr. Glover. The rest of you follow right behind us. If I turn around, I want to see fourteen of you there. Are we ready?"

They were, and the parade down the platform began. When they reached the end of the last coach, Charles Glover turned toward the tracks.

"Isn't town the other way, Mr. Glover?" Riley called from the back of the line. Before Charles could answer, a clown ran across the rails toward them. The children stopped, and their mouths dropped open in surprise.

"Welcome! Welcome, everybody, to the circus!" He called. "Right this way, ladies and gentlemen! Come to the Big Top for the grandest show on earth!"

"Maybe Simon did see something," Bert whispered to Ethan. "We better keep a closer eye on him from now on."

The children rounded the railroad coach and were met with an astonishing sight. The sides of the freight cars were lifted, and rows of cages revealed the animals that Simon had seen the night before. In front of the cages stood another clown and two very small ladies, dressed in tights and little skirts.

"Meet Jacko the clown, Madam Mona, and Miss Carmen," their escort said. "I am Rudolfo, your ringmaster. Now, on with the show!"

Never, in their most fantastic dreams, could anyone have ever imagined the things they saw before them. These amazing folks made a pyramid by standing on each other's shoulders, rode a bicycle through a burning hoop, found coins behind the children's ears, and performed every kind of acrobatic trick ever seen. The animals roared and trumpeted and growled to add to the noise and circus atmosphere.

When the show ended, every child shook hands with the performers and received a bag of peanuts and candy. They walked back to the Orphan Train dizzy with excitement.

"They'll not sleep tonight," Matron predicted happily. "Wasn't that the nicest thing that could have happened?"

"It was," Charles agreed. "They'll never forget it. Now we'll have to watch to see that no one runs away to join the circus!"

Simon was the hero of the evening.

"I should have believed you," Ethan said to him. "You never told stories before. But it's hard to believe something you never see yourself."

The children waved good-bye to the circus train after supper, and a short time later, the Orphan Train headed west again, carrying sixteen children toward lives as unimaginable to them as a circus train.

9

A RUMOR DENIED

Rain poured down the windows of the Orphan Train, and
Ethan, watching it, recalled that he and Simon, Alice, and
Will had traveled toward Briarlane on just such a day as this
a year ago. They hadn't known where they were going then,
either.

"Bert, do you remember when you came to Briarlane?"

"Sort of," Bert replied. "I don't know who took me there,
but I knew I was only going to stay a couple of days until my
ma and pa came back." He rested his chin on the windowsill
and watched the rain. "It's been a long couple of days."

"Do you still think they'll be back?"

"Naw. Not really. I like to pretend they will. But I guess
it won't happen." Bert looked at Ethan and grinned. "I
suppose when I get my new home, I'll pretend I'm going
back to the orphanage again to work with Otis on the farm.
I wonder why we always want what we ain't got?"

"I guess you like what you know better than what you don't know," Ethan decided. "Don't you wonder what kind of folks your new ones will be?"

"Yeah. But I have a chance to look them over before I go with them. Yours have already spoken for you. What if you don't like them?"

"I don't know any people I don't like," Ethan replied. "There's some I like better than others, but you can get to like anybody if you have to. Besides, there's four of us, and we got each other."

Bert jumped up on the seat and reached overhead where his belongings were stored. "Yeah—and right now you got me, too. Let's play checkers."

The train steamed toward the next small town that was expecting them.

"Chelsea," Charles replied when Matron inquired what that town might be. "Not very big, but we had several inquiries from there." He looked out the window. "This storm may keep a lot of people away, though."

It did seem that they were running into rainy weather rather than away from it. Nevertheless, the children prepared themselves to meet anyone who might have ventured out. When the train stopped several hours later, faces pressed against the glass for a sight of the station. There was nothing to be seen.

"I don't think they got any town here," Philip declared. "I don't even see a station house. You sure this is the place?"

"There's a town," Charles told him. "You can't see it

through the downpour. I'll get out and find someone who knows where we go."

Charles pulled on a slicker and stepped out onto the platform. He returned in a moment, followed by a large man whose hair and mustache dripped water over his collar. The two men stood in the space between the cars, and Matron and the children could hear their conversation clearly.

"Name's McCarty. I'm the sheriff here, and I came down to tell you that your train ain't stopping in Chelsea."

"I don't understand. This place is on our schedule." Charles Glover dug a paper from his inner pocket and showed it to the sheriff. The man glanced at it and shook his head.

"Don't make no difference. This town don't hold with selling children."

"Selling children! That is certainly not what we're about. We're trying to find—"

Sheriff McCarty didn't allow Charles to finish his sentence. "We know what you're doing. We heard all about it from a place up north. Come from Chicago, didn't you?"

"Yes, but—"

"That's what I thought. You're one of those outfits that kidnaps children from the streets, then puts them on a train and sells 'em to farmers along the way. We don't want any part of that in Chelsea. If you wasn't passing through here, I'd arrest you and take you in. All's I can do is not let you off the train."

Agent Glover was upset, but he spoke as calmly as he

could. "You are mistaken, sir. I don't know where you got that information, but it is not correct. These children are available for adoption from a Christian orphanage and social service home. Not one of them has come against his will."

"Who's going to adopt a little ragamuffin off the street? What do we know about where they came from? Maybe they'll give our kids diseases. Nobody here wants them."

Matron had heard enough. She stepped over to the doorway and faced this visitor.

"Our children are as clean as any child in your town," she said. "And not one of them is sick. Why don't you come in and look for yourself?"

The sheriff looked ashamed as he snatched his hat from his head and answered Matron.

"No offense, ma'am. I was just reporting what some folks in town was saying."

He looked over her shoulder at the children, staring wide-eyed at this unusual occurrence. They were once again scrubbed clean, brushed, and dressed in their best clothes. A look of surprise crossed Sheriff McCarty's face, and he entered the car with Charles Glover.

"These here are nice-looking children," he muttered. "They don't look like ruffians. Maybe those folks that complained didn't know what they were talking about." The sheriff cleared his throat. "You may be right about them coming from a home, but how about the report that you're getting money for bringing them out here? If folks have to pay you in order to take one home, that's the same as selling them."

"We don't receive money, I assure you. The train coaches are provided by the Children's Aid Society in New York. The other expenses are covered by contributions to the homes. All we ask is that a child be cared for as one of the family, given an education, religious training, and brought up to be a good citizen. If a child or the new family is unhappy with the situation, we'll find the child another home."

"Sounds straight to me," the sheriff declared. "I'll have a talk with the folks. Seems like it might be better if the ones that are interested would come out here to the coach to see them. We wouldn't want one of these little 'uns to be washed away."

He turned and left, promising to return with others in a short while. The children, who had listened silently to the conversation, all wanted to talk at once.

"Was he really a sheriff? Did he have a gun?"

"He was a sheriff, all right. I'm sure he has a gun somewhere. He probably didn't think he'd need it here," Charles said.

"I hope he comes back and chooses me," Philip declared. "I'd help him fight the Indians!"

"Indians!" Shala was indignant. "There aren't any Indians out here to fight now, are there, Mr. Glover?"

"Well, there probably aren't a lot of wild ones around any longer. I wouldn't say they'd be Sheriff McCarty's biggest problem," Charles answered.

"Besides," Shala continued, "maybe he'd rather have a girl. Did you ever think of that?"

"I don't know what for," Bert put in. "Girls wouldn't be any help shooting bad guys or catching rustlers."

"Shala would!" Trudy spoke up. "She can do anything the boys can do—and probably better, too. You think you're so smart, but what does boys know?"

"Here, here," Matron interrupted. "Let's not have a war between the boys and the girls. I think you all do well at taking care of yourselves. Why don't we let our new families decide what you can do or not do?"

It wasn't long before several of the townsfolk appeared and boarded the Orphan Train. They were a friendly bunch of people, and to the delight of the children, they had all brought baskets of food.

"Thought we'd have a picnic for supper," one of the ladies announced. "We were planning to have it outside if the weather was fine." She beamed at the children as she sank down on a seat.

"We was real disappointed when we heard that the sheriff had word not to let you off the train," she confided to Matron. "Some folks up north of here heard rumors about this train, but Sheriff McCarty says he doesn't think they're true. So we went ahead and came. My name's Naomi Pruitt."

Mrs. Pruitt settled back in the seat and patted the red plush covering beside her. "My, ain't these nice? I never been on a train in my life. How does it feel to be hurtled along through space that way? Scary, huh?"

"We've gotten used to it," Matron replied. "We've certainly met some interesting people." She smiled at Mrs.

Pruitt. "It was lovely of you to think of a picnic. We'll all enjoy it."

"Mercy, yes. I can't sit here and visit. I'd better get this food set out. More folks are on the way."

By the time everyone had arrived, the coach was crowded with visitors and children. Four seats were needed to contain all the wonderful things the ladies had prepared. The children were struck speechless with the display of ham and chicken and turkey on big platters. Bowls of potato salad, baked beans, coleslaw, and pickles sat beside the rolls, butter, and jam. Cakes, pies, cookies, and fruit completed the meal.

"I never saw that much to eat in my whole life," Trudy declared. "Do you suppose they get to have all this every day?"

"I wouldn't be surprised," Matron replied. "Country folks work hard and eat well."

"I'd work hard too, for food like this," Trudy said. "I hope someone takes me home with them."

Naomi Pruitt put her arm around Trudy's shoulder.

"I'll take you with me," she said. "I never saw such a skinny young one. My children will love to have a new sister in the family."

Trudy's eyes sparkled, and she hugged Mrs. Pruitt tightly. "How many children do you have?" she asked.

"Only eight," Mrs. Pruitt said, "and they're all older than you are. You'll be the only one in school. Except of course your sister Dary. She's the teacher. What grade you in?"

Trudy looked troubled. "I ain't never been to school."

"Well, don't you worry about that. Dary'll have you

reading in no time. You just get together whatever you got to take with you."

"Look!" Philip called from the window. "Here comes the sheriff back, and he's got a lady with him. Do you suppose he came for one of us?"

Sheriff McCarty answered that question when he and his wife joined the others. "We don't plan to adopt anyone," he said to Charlie Glover, "but my wife Rose here wanted to see the train and the children. Never had anything like this in town before. Guess that's why I was suspicious. Nothing personal, you understand."

"Of course," Charles replied. "You were wise to be cautious. I'll leave an address that you can use to check things out if you have any questions."

"Ask him if he carries a gun," Bert whispered to Ethan.

"You ask him," Ethan replied. "You're not afraid of anyone."

"I'll ask him," Philip volunteered. "Maybe I'll even ask him if he'd like to take me." He sidled over to the big man.

"Mr. Sheriff, sir. Us fellows would like to see your gun."

"Well, now, I'm sorry, son. I didn't expect to meet any bad guys on this train, so I left the gun back in my office."

"That's all right," Philip told him. "Someday I'll have one of my own. I'm going to be a sheriff when I grow up."

Sheriff McCarty looked around the car, then called to a man who was talking to a neighbor. "Here, Cal. Here's a young fellow who wants to be a deputy. What do you think?"

Cal came over and looked at Philip. "That's my

brother," the sheriff said. "And he's looking to find a boy that might make a good lawman."

Philip found his hand lost in the big one belonging to Cal McCarty, and his arm shaken vigorously.

A loud voice boomed out, "How old are you?"

"Eight."

"You ever been in jail?"

"No, sir," Philip gulped.

"Good place to stay out of. You like school, do you?"

"Yes, sir."

"Looks like a pretty good deputy to me," Cal said to his brother. "Let's see what Emma thinks."

Emma McCarty agreed, and Philip was ready to leave happily to begin a new life in Chelsea.

The sheriff's wife, Rose, was talking with Matron as she looked around the coach. "Brandon was right," she said. "These are lovely children. Do you think all of them will . . ." Suddenly Rose turned pale and stopped speaking.

Matron watched her with alarm. "Are you all right, Mrs. McCarty? You look ill. Do sit down!"

Sheriff McCarty hurried over to his wife. "What's the matter, Rose? What happened?"

Rose pointed. "That's Kathleen's girl!"

Matron turned to see who the woman was talking about. "That's Shala. She's one of our girls."

"She does look like your sister Kathleen, all right, but your sister was never in Chicago. And anyway," the man reminded his wife, "we know that the family died in a fire."

"But Brandon, no one could look that much like

Kathleen and not be her daughter." Rose turned to Matron
Daly. "Was she found on the streets of Chicago?"

"Oh, no," Matron replied. "Shala has been at Briarlane
Christian Children's Home since she was two years old.
That was eleven years ago."

"Where is the home?" Sheriff McCarty asked.

"In Pennsylvania. Shala was brought in by a woman
who said the child's parents had died in an accident. The
name on her baptismal certificate was Shala O'Brien."

"It is Kathleen's baby!" Rose declared. "Oh, Brandon—
they told us the whole family was gone! But I knew the
moment I saw her that she had to be Kathleen's girl!"

"It certainly looks like it," her husband said. "She's our
girl now."

Together they went to talk with Shala, and soon they
were getting her things in a bag to take with her.

"I found a family that was really family!" Shala
exclaimed. "I didn't know anyone in the world belonged to
me!"

"Chances are you wouldn't know it now if I hadn't
heard those rumors," Sheriff McCarty said.

"Oh! What if you had sent the train on without ever
knowing that our Shala was on there!" Rose hugged Shala
again. "But the Lord knew. He turned something bad into
good for us."

There were hugs and tears when the three children
finally left with their new families.

"How are we going to get along without Shala bossing
us around?" Bert wondered aloud that evening.

"She could play ball better than some of the boys," Riley reflected.

"Yeah, and marbles, too," Ethan added. "And she took good care of Alice."

Everyone was quiet as the train pulled away from Chelsea. Of the twenty-five orphans who had left Chicago, thirteen were left.

"It gets to feel a little lonesome as we get toward the end of our route," Charles Glover said to Matron. "They're glad when their friends find new homes, but they can't help wondering what lies ahead for them."

"I've worked with homeless children most of my life," Matron said, "and I don't think there's a braver bunch anywhere to be found. I've tried to give all of them the hope that there is one Friend who will be with them, no matter where they go. Sometimes it's sad to see little people have to grow up so fast."

She looked over at Ethan, who held Will in his lap as they looked at a book together.

"I'm grateful that you've given a Bible to every child as he leaves. Who knows what harm that will keep them from."

"The Bibles are a gift from a gentleman in Chicago who is interested in Hull House," Charles replied. "It's the only possession some of these children have when they leave us. I'm sure God will honor that."

He will indeed, Matron thought later as she made sure the girls were covered for the night. *Whatever their future holds, God is in it.*

10

THE MESSENGER
OF HOPE

By the time the Orphan Train chugged into Sioux City,
all the Chicago children had been adopted, placed in
Glidden, Vail, and Mapleton.

"Looks like there's just us now," Riley commented as
they left the last little town behind. "Us" included Riley,
Bert, and the four Coopers.

"Bert here needs to find a home," Riley continued. "It
won't matter so much about me. I can apprentice
somewhere even if there is no family that wants me. I'm old
enough to be on my own."

Riley's voice was wistful as he spoke, and the others knew
that he really longed for parents of his own who would give
him more than a job to do. Ethan recalled the picture of the
young woman that he had found on the floor near Riley's
bed, when they were living at Briarlane. It had been Riley's
mother, and Ethan knew that he treasured the picture.

"What do you want to do, Riley? Who you going to apprentice to?" Bert was curious. "I wish I was old enough to do that. But I guess I still have to go to school."

"I've been thinking on it," Riley replied. "I'd like to do something to help people, like Mr. Glover does. But maybe there's not much call for boys in that kind of business."

"There's always room for a boy who likes people and wants to help them," Charles assured him. "It may mean that you'll need another trade too, and maybe even go to school. But the world can't have too many who are willing to spread the good news of the Gospel and work to make things better. I think you've made a good choice."

"Yes, Riley," Matron said, "you're just the kind of boy who's needed in that work. I couldn't have handled all these children without your help. We'll pray about a special place for you."

"I guess I'll do whatever my new folks want me to," Ethan said. "I know I'll learn to be a good farmer."

"And Alice will be a good housekeeper," Matron added as she hugged the little girl to her. "Your family can't help but love all of you."

"What would you like to do if you could choose anything, Ethan?" Bert asked.

"I'd probably be an artist. I like to put what I see on paper."

"You like to put it on pigs, too," Bert reminded him. "Remember how you whitewashed the hog last year?"

Ethan nodded and pulled his drawing book from the overhead rack. "I drew it so I wouldn't forget."

The others looked at the picture and laughed. The huge pig lay on his side, sound asleep, while Ethan held a brush, dripping with whitewash, over his back.

"I remember that, too," Matron said. "What I recall best is scrubbing you boys clean after that day's business. But you're an excellent artist, Ethan. You must continue to draw, even if it isn't to be your life's work."

The train spent part of a day in Sioux City, the last stop in Iowa. Matron fixed a lunch that they could carry with them, and while Charles shopped, she and the children set out to explore the city. They hadn't gone far when they found a lovely green park on the banks of the Floyd River.

"Here's a place!" Riley exclaimed. "We can play stickball, and everyone has lots of room to run."

Matron agreed, and settled herself in the sun on the riverbank. Alice and Will fed the ducks with a piece of bread from the lunch bag while the older boys raced each other from tree to tree. The day was beautiful with a bright blue sky and fluffy clouds scuttling from the west.

Later, Riley lay on his back and watched the clouds as they rested for a few minutes. "I wonder if Nebraska is as pretty as this," he said.

"I'm sure it will have a beauty all its own," Matron answered. "I understand there's lots of prairie out there, and not many cities. Mr. Glover says even the small towns are far apart."

"I suppose folks get lonesome if they don't have close neighbors," Bert said. "If I'm going to live out there, I hope

I can have me a horse. I'll need one to come visit you, Ethan."

"The longer we're together on the train, the closer we'll live to each other," Ethan said. "Maybe we'll be close enough to walk."

When the boys suggested this to Charles that evening, the agent wasn't so sure. "In Nebraska you can't walk between farms, let alone towns," he told them. "There are miles and miles of land that has nothing on it but prairie grass. Farmers own sheep and cattle that have never been near a house."

The boys had trouble imagining anything that desolate. "You better like the folks you live with if they're all you're going to see," Bert commented. "I guess you'd have to have a horse to go to school and church. I think when I grow up I'd like to have a newspaper so people can read about what their neighbors are doing."

"That sounds like a worthy career," Matron said. "You'd make a good newspaperman, Bert. You always know what's going on."

By evening, when the train moved on, the wind was beginning to blow hard. The children watched from the windows, fascinated by the big tumbleweeds that rolled along by the train.

"Some of those things are as tall as I am!" Riley exclaimed. "They're picking up pieces and getting bigger all the time. That wind could blow you over!"

The next morning they awoke to a world that none of them had ever seen before. The sun was visible as a bright spot in the east sky, but there was no way to tell where the sky and the land met. Dust and sand blew against the windows, and the children couldn't see beyond the train tracks.

"I think I'm chewing sand," Simon complained. "It's all over my seat, too. How does it get in through the windows?"

"Dust storms like this are common in Nebraska," Charles told him. "No matter how tight the doors and windows are, it blows in. You'll be chewing it for a while until we get through this storm."

"Wow!" Ethan called. "Look at this! This stuff is going around in a circle and straight up off the ground!"

"That's called a 'dust devil,' " Charles told him. "There's so much open space that the earth is picked up in a whirlwind. We can be thankful that we aren't out in that. People have gotten lost in dust storms. It's impossible to see where you're going."

"I can imagine what a cleaning job there would be after one of those," Matron put in. She picked up a blanket by the corner, then dropped it back on the seat. "I'd better not shake that or we'll be as bad off as they are outdoors. How long do these storms last?"

"Sometimes for days," Charles replied, "but we may be heading out of this one. I hope so, because sometime tomorrow we're due in the little town of Kelsey. We'll stay overnight there. Then in another two days, we'll be in Willow Creek. That's where your new family is, Ethan. I imagine they're anxious for you to arrive."

The boys looked at each other soberly. Only three days left before they would be separated.

"I'm not ever going to forget you, Bert," Ethan said. "You're my best friend in the whole world."

"Just wait," Bert declared. "When we're grown up, with our own families, we can have farms right next to each other. We'll always be friends."

The little group awoke the next morning in a town so small that one could see all of it without moving away from the tiny railroad depot. A general store with a post office inside, a blacksmith shop, a tavern, and a school were the prominent buildings. Several small sod houses could be seen in the distance, but most of the area was bare and brown, like the country they had been riding through.

"Well, we can't lose anybody here," Bert declared. "You can see anything that moves, it's so flat. I'm glad Pete got adopted before now. He sure wouldn't find anything to hide behind in this place."

"I don't think there's anything to hide from," Riley commented. "At least we've come out of that dust storm, or we wouldn't be able to see this much."

"Let's have breakfast," Matron suggested, "then you may all go exploring on your own. I won't need to go with you today. You'll come back when you're hungry."

Although there was no danger in Kelsey, the children did stay together as they walked through the little town. As was expected, the residents who saw the unfamiliar troupe of five boys and a girl were curious as to who the strangers might be.

Some of the people wandered out to the railroad track to look over the Orphan Train. Matron invited them in, and later she reported to Charles and the children what had taken place.

"You mean these children is looking for homes?" The middle-aged lady was shocked. "Where's their folks?"

Matron explained as best she could, but the woman shook her head.

"No, I don't mean a pa and ma. I mean folks—grandmas and aunts and uncles and kin that's supposed to look after orphaned young 'uns. You mean they ain't got nobody blood to 'em?"

"Some of them have, but they just aren't able to care for a child. They don't have the room or the food."

This was hard for these country folk to comprehend.

"We ain't got hardly a family in Kelsey that ain't taking in someone that weren't born to 'em. We look after each other out here."

"But you're doing a good thing," another hastened to add. "Them poor little waifs wouldn't grow up to amount to much if you didn't help 'em. You're doing your Christian duty."

The others nodded in agreement. "We never heard of such before, but you're good people. Maybe you'd all have supper with us before the meeting."

"The meeting?"

"Yes'm. The chapel train is here this month, and we have a meeting every night. We'd be proud to have you come."

Charles nodded when Matron shared her news. "I saw the chapel car on a siding just beyond the station. I was going to go over and see what it was this afternoon."

"I'd like to go, too," Riley declared. "Have they made a church building out of a railroad car?"

"If they have, it sounds like a moving church to me," Matron said. "It will be fine to have some fellowship with folks this evening."

After dinner the younger boys and Alice chose to play ball and amuse themselves. Charles and Riley walked down the track to the ninety-foot car that, from the outside, looked like their own.

" 'The Messenger of Hope,' " Riley read as they approached it. "Sounds like a church, all right. Do you suppose there's someone here now?"

In answer to his question, a hearty voice boomed out the door. "Good afternoon, friends!"

The voice was followed by a jolly-looking man with a broad smile. He stretched out his hand to his two visitors.

"I see you moved in to share my track this morning. I was going to come and call on you, but you beat me to it. Dawson is the name. Rev. Oscar Dawson. Come in, come in."

The sight that met Charles and Riley was something that neither of them had ever seen before. Across the back third of the car hung a long, red curtain. They looked at it curiously.

"That's where we live," Rev. Dawson told them. "Mother, come and meet our visitors," he called.

From behind the curtain came a smiling woman, every bit as jolly-looking as her husband. "Welcome! We don't often see strangers in these little towns. Sit down and let me bring you some fresh cookies."

Mrs. Dawson scurried away, and while Charles Glover talked with the preacher, Riley looked around the car with interest. The red plush seats were like the ones he was used to, but the rest of the chapel car didn't look the same at all. As the sun shone through the window, bright splashes of color danced on the red plush seats and the floor, and Riley looked up to see that the tops of the transoms were made of stained glass. In place of the first two seats in front, there stood a potbelly stove. Beside it was a pulpit, an organ, and a small altar. Riley sank down and gazed at the miniature church surrounding him. The men's voices reached him, and he listened with great excitement.

"There are lots of homesteaders in this territory," Rev. Dawson said. "As you can see, houses are few and far between. Sometimes no more than eight or ten families live within driving distance of each other. Most often it's fewer than that, in fact."

"We noticed that there weren't a lot of people around. This must be hard country to settle." Charles looked out the window at the vast prairie surrounding them.

"It is indeed," the preacher agreed. "These good folks work hard and have very few of the necessities that people of large towns and cities take for granted. Generally, there are not enough families within a ten-mile radius to support a church and a pastor, but they still need to be spiritually fed."

"And that's where you come in," Charles said. "Tell me, how did this come about? I've never happened to run into a chapel car before. Are you the only one out here?"

"Oh, no." Rev. Dawson chuckled happily. "I believe there are nearly a dozen of us on the tracks here in the west. We were commissioned by the American Baptist Home Missionary Society when folks started moving into this new territory. The idea was, why not have a church that moves too? A car like this can serve as a church and a parsonage together, and use the tracks already laid."

Charles laughed. "Now that's good business! No taxes, no grounds to maintain, and very little upkeep on your building."

"Right. And if the preacher is run out of town, the engine hooks on and takes the church with him!"

The two men laughed heartily at the notion.

"That doesn't happen often, I can assure you," Rev. Dawson said. "The Lord has been good to us. We stay in a town like Kelsey here for a month or two, then a passing train will take us on and carry us to the next stop."

"And is this an expense that your mission society covers?"

"Doesn't cost a penny. The railroad provides the service free. Over the years a number of small churches have been formed where we've visited. We often stop for a week of meetings at places like this where there was nowhere to worship before we came through. Now they're becoming independent. Couldn't be a better missionary service than this."

Riley munched the cookies Mrs. Dawson brought to him and visited with her while the man discussed the affairs of the growing state of Nebraska.

"Doesn't seem quite fair," Mrs. Dawson mused. "Papa and I don't have any children to take care of and here you are—six nice children with no parents. My, that's a wonderful thing that these folks are taking you to new families. Do you remember your own parents?"

"Not very well," Riley replied. "I know my ma was pretty and young, but maybe that's because I have her picture." He drew it from his pocket and offered it to the preacher's wife. "I don't remember a pa or anyone else."

Mrs. Dawson studied the face and looked at Riley. "A lovely, sweet girl," she said. "You favor her. How good the Lord was to have you placed in a Christian home. I'll look forward to meeting your Matron this evening."

Riley was quiet as he and Charles walked back to the Orphan Train. He listened as the agent told the others about the chapel car, but he didn't say much except to tell Matron that Mrs. Dawson's cookies were almost as good as hers.

No one objected to being scrubbed up and dressed in their finest for the evening's outing. They watched eagerly as horses and buggies, people on horseback, and folks on foot came from all directions across the prairie.

"Where is everyone coming from?" Bert exclaimed. "There aren't that many houses for 'em to be out of!"

"Many of them have come from too far away for us to see their houses, even if this is flat land," Charles told him.

"But there are more homes near here than you would guess. A lot of them are still underground."

"Underground! You mean they live in a hole?" Ethan was startled.

"No, not a hole. Many of them begin to build by digging a big room for a basement later. They live there until they can afford to build the rest of the house. It's a perfect plan. It's easy to keep warm in the winter, and cool in the summer. The dust storms blow over the top of them. They only have to keep the chimney and fireplace openings free and clear. Most new settlers live in soddies while they homestead their land."

"How about that!" Bert said. "We been looking at people's houses and didn't even know it!"

The chapel car was nearly full when the service began. The little pump organ accompanied the hymns, and everyone sang joyfully. Rev. Dawson welcomed the orphans, and after the sermon, he prayed that each one of them would grow to trust God and do His will.

Ethan listened carefully. He had heard a lot about God in the past year, and he was sure that God loved him and would care for him.

When most of the people had left after the service, the preacher shook hands with Matron and Charles Glover, then with each of the children.

"God bless you in your new life," he said. "God will lead you if you allow Him to do so."

Riley had been unusually silent during the evening, but now he spoke up.

"Rev. Dawson, this kind of work is what I want to do. I want to serve God and the people who need Him."

The preacher looked at Riley carefully. "Son, do you believe that Jesus Christ is your Lord and Savior?"

"Yes, sir."

Rev. Dawson looked at his wife, and she nodded her head. "Then Mother and I would be pleased and proud to have you as a son. The Lord's work is our life, and if you want it to be your life too, this is the place for you."

Mrs. Dawson hugged Riley, and so did Matron. His eyes were bright and his smile wide as the group returned to their cars for the night.

The next morning the children waved to Riley, standing by the chapel car, until the "Messenger of Hope" was out of sight. No one wanted to talk about it, but with Riley gone they couldn't deny that the trip was almost over. Ethan and Bert stayed close together as the Orphan Train steamed on toward the center of Nebraska.

11

THE LAST STOP

The flickering lamp in the center of the wooden table gave enough light for Hannah to cut the biscuits and shove them into the oven. Through the open door she could see that the sun was shining and the day would be fine. No matter what the weather had looked like, the day would be fine, Hannah thought happily. In the distance she could hear Carl's joyous whistle. This was the day they had waited for since the announcement had been posted in Willow Creek three weeks ago. Today they would get a child!

Hannah brushed the flour from her hands and looked anxiously around the room. The door admitted the only outside light, and she could see just dim outlines of the furniture, but Hannah knew every inch of her home without looking. Large, smooth stones shored up the dirt walls. Hard clay sealed the cracks and covered the slightly uneven floor. The two back corners were separated from the rest of the room by long, bright red cretonne curtains.

Hannah smiled as she looked at them. They were certainly the brightest spot in the room. A wave of homesickness washed over her as she pictured her mother folding that heavy material into a box for the trip west.

"There's a lot here," Mama had said. "You can curtain every window in your new house and upholster the chairs with what's left over."

Hannah had never suspected, any more than Mama had, that her new house wouldn't even have windows to curtain! So the cretonne wasn't cut up, but became the walls for two small bedrooms. There were other splashes of color too. Bright patchwork quilts covered the beds. Rags of every hue had been used to braid the rugs that made vivid islands on the dirt floor. As she looked at them, Hannah recalled the day she had entertained her first visitor in her new home.

"Hello-oo! Anyone here?"

Startled, Hannah wiped her hands on her bright yellow apron and ran to the door of the soddy. She and Carl had been here nearly two months, and this was the first voice she had heard besides their own.

"Yes, yes!" she called, and hurried out into the brilliant sunlight. Jumping down from her wagon was a woman who looked about Hannah's age, although she could have been older. The hot prairie wind whipped her long skirt around her legs. Under a gray poke bonnet, Hannah could see a sun-browned friendly looking face. She hastened to greet the stranger.

"Come in! Oh, I'm so glad to see you. Would you like some cold buttermilk?"

"I can't think of anything that I'd like better," the woman replied. "Buck told me you folks were here, so I thought I'd better come and check you out."

She followed Hannah down the steps into the cool interior of the room. Hannah pulled a chair to the table and seated her guest, then hurried to dip buttermilk from a heavy metal container. A plate of cookies completed the preparations, and Hannah settled down to enjoy her visitor.

The woman had said nothing since she'd entered, and now she regarded Hannah with interest.

"Let me guess," she said. "You've come from somewhere in the south."

"Why, yes," Hannah replied. "But how can you tell?"

"The accent, for one thing. And the New England girls tend to be more practical than southerners. I know. I came from Boston. Southern belles are flighty."

Hannah was stunned. "I'm practical," she protested. "Carl and I planned carefully for this move. I think we've done well."

"Now don't get your temper up. I don't even know your name yet. And you don't know mine. I'm Ruth Buck. And I already told you that Buck and I came from Boston."

"I'm Hannah Boncoeur." Hannah was still a bit annoyed, but she would be civil. "We came from Louisiana."

"Boncoeur. 'Good heart.' That's a lovely name. Takes some living up to, doesn't it?"

Hannah warmed a bit to her visitor. Ruth was blunt,

but perhaps she could be a good friend.

"May I ask why you call your husband by his last name?" she inquired politely.

Ruth threw her head back and laughed heartily. "Yes, but you must never let on that I told you. His given name is Aloysius, and he hates it! Can't say as I blame him. He said he wouldn't have married me if I'd been called Hepzibah or some other impossible New England name. He likes things plain and simple."

The women laughed together over this, and from there on conversation came easily. When it was time for Ruth to leave, they were good friends and promised to see each other as often as possible. Hannah walked with Ruth to the wagon, and before her guest left, asked the question that had been bothering her.

"Why do you think I'm impractical?"

Ruth looked down at Hannah's apron. "The bright colors. Most women coming west brought grays or browns, because they tend not to show the soil so badly. I can see, though, that you would die out here without color. It's right for you."

If Ruth thought I was impractical then, now she must be thinking Carl is impossible, Hannah chuckled to herself. She hurried to get the biscuits from the oven as she heard her handsome, irrepressible husband heading toward the doorway, singing at the top of his voice.

"I dream of Hannah, with the light brown hair. . . . "

Carl bounded down the stairs and, grabbing Hannah around the waist, whirled her about the room in time with his music.

"Carl! Behave yourself! I'm all ready for the trip to town, and you're going to make me have to comb my hair again!"

"Oh, you love it. You know you do. Isn't this a glorious day? Let's thank the Lord for it."

They sat down at the table and bowed their heads.

"Lord, this day is ours only by Your mercy. It is Yours to guide and direct. It may be one of the most important days of our lives, because we're going to bring a child into our home. We trust You have the one for us coming this way right now. Prepare us to accept this child, and the child to accept us. We want to bring him up in your love and favor. Thank you for this day and this food. Amen."

Carl's eyes sparkled as he ladled sausage gravy over his biscuits and poured cream into his coffee.

"If the train is on time, we shouldn't have long to wait when we get to town. Adopting a child is just about like having one of your own, except we know it's coming at a decent time. Is it a boy or a girl? Does it have brown eyes or blue? I can hardly wait to see!"

Hannah smiled, but her eyes were troubled.

"I hope we're doing the right thing, Carl. Is it fair to take a child from a big city and bring it to this desolate spot where all you can see is prairie grass and sky? Won't a little one be terribly lonely?"

"I brought you from a big city to this desolate spot," Carl reminded her. "Aren't you happy?"

"You know I am. I love the open spaces and our home. And I have you."

"The child will have us. You know we thought and prayed about this before we agreed to take an orphan. The Lord has the right one for us, I've no doubt."

Any child would be fortunate to have you for a father, Hannah thought as she watched Carl finish his breakfast. She had no reason to worry.

The sky was clear with morning light as they followed the North Loup River south toward Willow Creek and the next milestone in their lives.

Ethan awoke in the night to hear the lonesome *whoo, whoo* as the Orphan Train apparently passed some little town or a road that crossed the tracks. Somehow the sound echoed louder and stayed in the air longer out here on the prairie. On the seat facing his, Bert slept soundly. Across the aisle Simon and Will didn't move. Ethan wasn't sure why he had awakened, but he remembered immediately that Riley was no longer there in the front of the car. He felt sad. The boys had depended on Riley to know just what to do and how to get around in strange places. They had talked it over the night before.

"I wonder if Riley will be able to sleep tonight in a railroad car that isn't moving," Bert said. "I think I'm going to figure that something's wrong if I wake up and my bed is still."

"Me, too," Ethan agreed. "It seems like we've been on this train forever." He looked around the nearly empty coach. "Remember when this place was full? Do you suppose all those guys are enjoying their new homes?"

Bert looked out the window at the bright stars. "They can see the same stars we can," he commented. "It makes you think maybe we didn't leave them so far behind. When we get lonesome for each other, we can look at the sky." He was silent for a moment, then he answered Ethan's question.

"Yeah, they'll enjoy them. Every place is about the same. You just have to get used to the people."

"If we both get left in Willow Creek, maybe we'll go to the same school," Ethan said. "That way we'll see each other every day. Do you suppose our folks will be acquainted?"

Charles Glover heard their question.

"Willow Creek is the only place to come for mail and supplies, so chances are they will," he said. "Of course, for some homesteaders it can be a half day's trip to get to town, so they may not go often. Some children out on the prairie are taught at home."

It was hard to imagine what the future held. Ethan, thinking it over in the night, couldn't picture what lay ahead for him and the others. He believed what Matron said, though, about the Lord going with them, so very soon he was asleep again.

The view from the window in the morning hadn't changed a lot. The land was flat, and today the sky was cloudless. As Matron prepared the breakfast, Simon stood and watched the passing scene.

"Those are sure funny-looking cows out there," he said finally. The others went to look.

"I don't think those are cows," Bert said. "Their heads are too big and they have long hair."

"Buffalo," Charles said when they called him to look. "They usually run in herds, so there are more around here somewhere."

"Do the farmers own them?" Ethan wanted to know.

"No, they run wild out here. The prairie is covered with 'buffalo grass.' It's called that because it's what the animals feed on. People hunt them, though. They have thick, tough hides that make good carriage robes and moccasins. The Indians use every part of the buffalo for something. Some of the animals are even tamed and used to work on a farm."

"Hey—I'd like to ride a buffalo," Bert said. "But they don't look like they'd move very fast."

"They don't now," Charles told him, "but if you ever saw a herd stampede, you'd see how fast they move. You wouldn't want to be in the way."

"I don't even want to be in the way of one of them," Ethan decided. "I hope there aren't any on the farm I'm living on."

"There probably won't be," Charles reassured him. "Chances are Mr. Rush works his place with horses, just the way they did at Briarlane."

"I don't even know that I'll be on a farm, do I?" Bert said. "I might live right in town, like Arthur and Shala do. It's kind of exciting not to know. Maybe I'm glad I don't."

Charles Glover looked at his watch. "You'll know before

too long. We should be in Willow Creek very soon after dinner. Do you all have your things together?"

Matron helped put their belongings in the bags they carried, and they went through their last scrubbing and brushing at her hands.

"Tomorrow my new mama will braid my hair," Alice said, "but she won't do it as good as you." She turned and hugged Matron tightly. "Can't you come and live there too?"

Matron held Alice close, and her eyes filled with tears. "The boys and girls back at Briarlane still need me," she said. "Your new mama will love you and take care of you just as I do. Besides, you'll have a new papa, too."

"I had a papa once," Alice replied. "I didn't like him much. But I'll try to like this one," she added quickly when she saw the sad look on Matron's face.

"Of course you will," Matron said. "Your folks and your big sister can't help but love all of you. Just remember what you've learned about Jesus. You can always pray to Him, no matter where you are. Now, you look fine." Matron patted the hair bow she'd just tied and turned her attention to Will.

This one will be spoiled, she thought. *He is a handsome little boy, and still young enough to be trusting of anyone who cares for him.*

Indeed, Will was happily unaware that his life was about to enter a new era. As long as his beloved sister and brothers were there, he had no fear for the future.

Ethan and Bert sat down to wait to the end of the trip. There didn't seem to be much to say, and both were busy with their thoughts. Ethan opened his bag and pulled out his drawing book.

"Here, Bert. I want you to have this to remember me. You can show the pictures to your folks and tell them about where you came from."

Bert's mouth dropped open, and he stared at Ethan with wide eyes.

"Your drawing book? What will you do without it? It's the best thing you have!"

"That's all right. I really want you to have it. Maybe I'll get another one. If not, I can draw in the dirt, like I used to. I'll always probably draw on something." He handed the book to Bert and settled back with a happy smile.

"I'll always keep it, Ethan, and someday we'll live close enough together to share it. I don't have anything great like that to give to you, but you can have this."

Bert stood up and dug deep in his pocket. He pulled out a chain, from which dangled a heavy key, and laid it in Ethan's hand.

"This was my pa's," Bert said proudly. "He told me that praying is the key to success, and this key would remind me of that when I need help. Now it's yours. Who knows when you'll have to get in someplace or out of someplace? That key could come in handy!"

Ethan looked at the object in his hand. "A key? Have you ever opened anything with it, Bert?"

"Well, no. I never found a door it would fit, but it feels good in your pocket. And Pa said if I carried it I'd never give up, 'cause it would remind me to pray."

"And you want me to have it?" Ethan said. "What will you have to remind you, then?"

Bert shrugged. "I can always put my hand in my pocket. If you can draw pictures in the dirt, I can remember." He pulled the checkerboard out of his bag. "Let's have a game, shall we? The time will go faster that way."

A couple of hours later, the Orphan Train began to slow down, and Alice, Simon, and Will ran to the windows to watch for the approaching station. Willow Creek was obviously an older town than Kelsey, for trees had been planted and houses could be seen in the distance. Bert and Ethan reluctantly put away their game and crossed the aisle to the window. The screech of the big wheels told them that it wouldn't be long before the depot would be in sight, as well as a number of people. Among those faces were the folks who would determine what the lives of Ethan, Bert, and the others would be like. Could they tell by looking at those people what lay ahead for them?

"I'd rather not look," Ethan said. "If I see someone I'd like to go with, and they turn out not to be here for me, I'll be disappointed. Or if I see one I don't want to go with and he did come for me, I'll feel even worse."

"Well, the thing to do, see," Bert told him, "is not to decide by how they look. Just think that everyone out there is going to be your next best friend. Then whoever takes you, you already like 'em! Remember the man I thought wouldn't like boys, and Arthur went with him? I was wrong—they were just right for each other."

The train finally shuddered to a halt, and the children

eagerly scanned the faces looking up toward the window. Most everyone was smiling happily, and one man was waving his arms in greeting.

"That one's your pa, Bert," Ethan said. "He can hardly wait for you to get here."

"How do you know that?"

"Because he looks just right for you. You can just tell that he likes boys. Anyway, he's the one I want to be yours."

They had no further time to discuss it, for Charles Glover opened the door and beckoned the children to follow him off the Orphan Train.

12

GOING HOME

The big house south of Willow Creek was alive with
activity early in the morning. The hired girl, Polly, had the
fires going before daybreak.

Polly could hardly be accurately described as a "girl,"
since she was every minute as old as Manda Rush. Neither, as
she told her ma on her infrequent days off, was she "hired"
for much.

"If it wasn't that we had to have money for you, I'd quit
that place in a hurry. Her highness thinks that if she gives
me her worn-out clothes, I'm well paid. I work as hard as
the men do, and I know she doesn't pay me all the mister
gives her for my wages."

Polly gave another vicious shake to the kitchen range
and grumbled to herself. "Four more children to look
after. I'd think one lazy young one around here would be
plenty. What are we starting here—an orphanage? Four

times more work and no more pay."

Her complaints carried to Luke and Henry as they washed up in the tin basin.

"One of 'em is a gal, ain't she? Maybe you can get some help in the kitchen," Luke suggested.

"Hmph," Polly snorted. "How much help can you get from a six year old?" She paused with the spatula in the air and considered. "Come to think of it, I was working in the kitchen when I was that age. Peeled vegetables and slopped the hogs and took care of the chickens. Maybe she could be useful. Never will get that good-for-nothing Frances to do anything on the place."

The men sat down at the table and accepted the huge stack of flapjacks and platter of ham and eggs set before them. Henry bowed his head and prayed silently while Luke shoveled the food into his mouth with vigor.

"The oldest boy can soon get into the milking and weeding." Luke poured syrup on his plate and sopped it up with a flapjack. "The rest of 'em's too young to be much good."

"Maybe they'll bring a little happiness to the place," Henry suggested. "Been pretty quiet around here since Robbie's gone."

"Quiet for you," Polly said, "but it ain't been quiet in here. 'Polly, do this; Polly, come and help me. Isn't that finished yet, Polly?' Regular slave driver, she is. I don't see much advantage to adding four more to this kettle."

Out in the barnyard, Chad Rush was closing the gate on
the last of the milk cows. He paused to watch as they ambled
toward the pasture, then let his gaze shift to the horizon.
Land as far as he could see in any direction belonged to him.
As he watched the sky lighten in the east, he imagined that
he could hear a train whistle. He couldn't, of course. But he
knew exactly when the train would come through Willow
Creek today, and he knew what it brought to him.

If only he and Manda could agree on something and work
together, life would be easier. Manda had many good points,
he supposed, but on matters of child rearing the two of them
were far apart. His wife was short-tempered and her patience
almost nonexistent. If a child disobeyed or annoyed her,
punishment was swift. There was no thinking it over or
planning ahead. On the other hand, if Manda felt life was
going her way and she was in a good mood, the same behavior
brought no punishment. Little Robbie had learned to sidestep
the bad times and take advantage of the good ones.

As he walked slowly toward the house, Chad admitted
to himself that his attitude toward children was the same as
his father's had been toward him. It had not been easy to
grow up under the heavy hand of the older man, but he was
the better for it. As Chad looked around the neat farm with
its well-cared-for buildings, he recalled the strappings he
had endured before he learned to do a job well, and without
complaining. How old was the boy coming today? Eight?
Nine? Not too young to begin training in the way he should
go. From past experience Chad knew that Manda wouldn't
allow him to discipline the younger boys, especially not the

baby. But they would grow up in time.

Chad splashed water on his face and ran wet hands through his hair. He knew his Christian duty, and he would do it. "Train up a child in the way he should go, and when he is old, he will not depart from it," the Good Book said. Chad was living proof that this was an accurate proverb, and he intended to begin at once to show these children the importance of obedience.

In the kitchen, Manda was assisting Polly to get breakfast on the table for the family, but her loud complaints were directed toward Frances.

"You're the one who absolutely had to have a sister, and now you don't want her in your room! Where do you expect her to sleep—in the barn?"

"There's enough rooms in this house so everyone can have their own," Frances replied. "She isn't even half my age. She'd be into my things all the time."

"Each in a room of his own? And just who is going to wash all that extra bedding, missy?"

"Polly."

A sudden thud of the skillet on the stove top expressed the opinion of that listener, and Manda glanced at Polly's stormy-looking face.

"Polly will have enough to do without cleaning extra rooms," Manda told the girl. "You have no idea how much more work four children will be." She looked at Frances sharply. "It wouldn't hurt you to take on a little of it."

"You forget that I have to go to school and study and practice my organ lessons. How much time do you think I have anyway?"

"Now, look here. . . ." Manda began, but she was interrupted by the slam of the back screen door.

"Frances, don't argue with your mother," Chad said.

"She thinks I should let that girl share my room," Frances complained.

"You're the one who said you wanted a sister," Chad reminded her. "You insisted on taking all four children."

"The director of the home said we had to take them all," the girl answered sullenly. "I wanted the little one to take Robbie's place. I don't care about the others. You can give them to someone else."

"There, see?" Manda couldn't hide her triumph. "I told you what would happen if you gave in to her every whim. I knew you'd pay for it one day. Well, it seems like that day has come."

Chad ignored her and answered Frances. "If we turn the others over to someone else, we'll lose the little one, too. You'd better make up your mind before we get to town."

"I'll think of something," Frances declared. "They can stay out of my way if they all come here."

As Chad finished his breakfast, he contemplated the days that lay ahead. He had not yet mentioned to Manda or Frances that he'd filed a record on the land in South Dakota. They would be required to live on it for a year and cultivate the property. He'd intended to tell Manda his plans before now, but the time just hadn't been right. The longer he waited, the greater the furor would be. As soon as the business of this day was over, he'd do it.

The hired men, Luke and Henry, stood at the barn door as the Rushes' buggy turned on the road toward town. Luke shook his head. " 'Fraid we're all going to rue this day's work," he said. "Don't know what possessed Chad to take on four orphans."

"I suppose he thinks it's his Christian duty," Henry offered. "Bible says to look after the widows and orphans. He certainly has enough money to look after quite a few."

"Chad's heavy on duty, all right, but you and me don't see eye to eye on the 'Christian.' I'd hate to be one of those kids."

"Chad's not a real lovable sort," Henry agreed, "but he does what he thinks the Bible tells him to. His pa never spared the rod on him, I've heard."

"I can see whackin' a boy to get his attention if he really needs it. Some boys are hard to handle. I can't see makin' 'em buckle under just so's you can be boss, though."

Henry pondered this silently. "Chad wouldn't be able to stand a strong-minded boy. He has a way of making you feel a little lower than he is. These boys will have to think his way or pay for it. Now me, I'd rather have the strap and my pride. But then," he concluded, "I'm not his son. I can walk away if I feel like it."

"Best we get to work," Luke suggested. "They'll be back here before suppertime."

In Willow Creek the stationmaster consulted the timetable for the exact arrival time of the westbound train. Ed Swartz from over near Hawley stood at the ticket window and waited. Sam pushed his glasses up on his nose and ran a stubby finger down the column in front of him.

"Two-fourteen," he announced. "Should be on time. Expecting someone, are you, Ed?"

Ed shifted from one foot to the other and looked pained. " 'Fraid so. The missus sent me in to get one of them orphans."

He glanced out toward the platform where a number of people had already gathered, although more than an hour remained before the train was due. "Won't hurt my feelings none if there ain't enough to go around. We just got our last one off the place and she wants to start over."

"Morton, back at Kelsey, says there's five young 'uns left on the train," Sam informed him. "Doubt we have that many families looking to take one. They left just one boy in Kelsey. Only other family here in town bent on getting an orphan as I've heard of is Edith and Ned Watkins. Might be more from the country."

Ed nodded dismally. "I was afraid of that. I'll stand back until everyone else has had their pick." He leaned on the counter and continued to survey the group outside.

"I see Chad and Manda Rush came in. Are they really looking to take another orphan?"

"Yep. So's I hear. You know how closedmouth he is, but we heard him say he was thinking on it. Don't know as I'd try again if I was him."

"I'd rather see my Rilla bring one up than that Rush

woman," Ed declared. "Course, wasn't her fault the little fellow died, I guess. It's just that she doesn't seem like a child-loving person."

"There's all kinds of God-fearing folks around," Sam said. "It's just that some of 'em ain't as warmhearted as others. One thing about Chad, he'll leave them well-fixed. Hear tell he's filed claim up in South Dakota."

Several ladies had gathered on the platform to visit. Manda Rush wasn't among them. She stood tight-lipped off to the side, beside an unhappy-looking Frances.

"We ought to ask Manda to join us," the minister's wife suggested. "I don't want her to think we're talking about her."

"Well, we are," Edith Watkins pointed out. "If she was standing here we wouldn't be. You're right. We should ask her."

No one, however, made a move to go over to where the Rushes were standing. Hannah Boncoeur watched Manda with interest. "Why has she come for a child if she doesn't really want one, I wonder?"

"They lost a little boy two years ago," Edith told her. "I think the girl wanted one to take his place."

"Then she ought to look happy. I hope the boy is too little to know that they haven't counted the days until he got here, like we have." Hannah smiled with delight as she thought of the child they would take back with them. "I know that Carl would like a boy to work with him. A girl would be lots of company for me, but I guess I'd feel easier about a boy riding back and forth to school alone. So whatever the Lord sends, I'm going to be happy!"

Louisa Finch, the schoolteacher, smiled at her. "Your new child will be too," she said. "Children know when they're wanted. I don't know how old they all are, but I should have some of them in school by fall."

The stationmaster's wife spoke up. "Don't think you'll have the Rushes' boy, no matter how old he is. Sam says they're . . ."

A distant train whistle interrupted her sentence as all eyes turned toward the track. Everyone surged to the edge of the platform and watched as puffs of black smoke appeared on the horizon.

The first chug of the engine could be heard, and Hannah ran over to clutch Carl's arm tightly. Carl grinned broadly and waved his arms in the air. Then they waited breathlessly as the huge locomotive steamed up to the station house, and the two Orphan Train cars ground to a stop in front of them.

Agent Charles Glover stepped off to greet the waiting folk of Willow Creek, Nebraska. He was followed by Matron, carrying Will and holding Alice by the hand. Behind her, Ethan and Bert jumped down, pulling Simon between them.

"There's five," someone said.

"And only one girl. I wonder who will get her?"

"I'm sure that littlest one goes to Chad Rush."

They stood back and waited for Agent Glover to speak.

"Good afternoon." Charles paused and looked around. "Is Mr. Rush here?"

Chad stepped forward. "I am."

Charles smiled confidently. "Here's your family, sir."

Chad didn't smile. "There are five children here."

Mr. Glover put his hand on Bert's shoulder. "This boy isn't one of them. The other four are the Coopers."

Chad glanced at them and nodded. "All right. Come on."

Edith Watkins gasped in surprise. "You mean they're taking all of them? There's only one boy left!"

"Yes, ma'am. That's the arrangement that was made at the request of the Cooper family and the Home. The children have to stay together."

This announcement was not met with silence. Alice and Simon looked from one grown-up to the other while Ethan studied the man who was to be his father. He would wait until Mr. Glover told them to go before he left the safety of Matron and Bert.

Carl Boncoeur came to the front. "Has anyone spoken for this young man?" he asked, and put his arm around Bert's shoulder.

"We expect to get an orphan," Edith said. "We heard there were plenty to go around."

"Ed Swartz come for one, too," someone said. "But most of us has children at home, and we can do without if they're all taken care of."

Hannah stood on the other side of Bert, and she put her arm around him protectively also. "Who is going to get him, sir?" she asked anxiously.

The crowd waited for Charles to speak. He looked at Edith, then at the Boncoeurs and Bert.

"I believe this is a case where the boy should make a choice," he said. "Bert?"

Bert looked at Ethan and grinned. "Someone already made the best choice for me," he said.

He shook hands politely with Edith. "Thank you, ma'am, for wanting me. But these here are my folks." He beamed at Carl and Hannah. Hannah hugged him with tears on her face, and to the boys' great delight, Carl leaped into the air, waved his hat and shouted "Whoopee!"

In the background, Ed Swartz wiped his face with a big red handkerchief and sighed with relief.

Ethan pounded Bert on the back. "You got a pa who will dance a jig on the platform, Bert! Good for you!"

"Well," Edith said complacently. "There'll be other trains by, I'm sure. The next one may have our child. I'm glad to see everyone so happy."

Matron hugged each child in turn, and as Chad waited impatiently, Ethan said good-bye to Bert. With a promise from Carl and Hannah that the boys would see each other soon, Ethan's heart lifted a bit

Chad Rush spoke. "Well, are you ready to go?"

Ethan turned and grasped Will and Simon by the hand. "Yes, sir. Come on, Alice."

The children followed Chad Rush to the buggy where Manda and Frances were already seated. Matron watched a moment, then hurried to take Alice's hand and walk with them.

"Mrs. Rush? I'm Matron Daly from Briarlane. These are good children. I hope you'll be happy together."

"Thank you, Matron," Manda answered stiffly. "They will have everything they need."

Everything but love, Matron thought. *God will have to provide that.* She waved as the buggy pulled away, then went back to join Charles at the station.

"Ethan is strong, Matron," Charles said to her. "They won't break his spirit. I expect great things of that boy."

In the buggy, Ethan thrust his hand deep into his pocket and felt Bert's key. He smiled as he answered Simon's question.

"Yes, we are, Simon. We're going to our home now."

Other books by Arleta Richardson

In Grandma's Attic
More Stories from Grandma's Attic
Still More Stories from Grandma's Attic
Treasures from Grandma
Sixteen and Away from Home
Eighteen and On Her Own
Nineteen and Wedding Bells Ahead
At Home in North Branch
New Faces, New Friends
Stories from the Growing Years
Christmas Stories from Grandma's Attic
The Grandma's Attic Storybook
The Grandma's Attic Cookbook

The Orphans' Journey Book One: Looking for Home
The Orphans' Journey Book Two: Whistle-stop West